The Coyotes Forgive You

The Coyotes Forgive You

STORIES

BY

JIM DRUMMOND

MONGREL EMPIRE PRESS
NORMAN, OKLAHOMA, UNITED STATES OF AMERICA

Norman, Oklahoma

2011

FIRST EDITION, 2011

The Coyotes Forgive You © 2011
by Jim Drummond

ISBN 978-0-9833052-1-7

Cover Image: *The Crucified Land* © 1939 by Alexandre Hogue from the collection of the Gilcrease Museum, Tulsa, OK. Used by permission.

MONGREL EMPIRE PRESS
NORMAN, OK

ONLINE CATALOGUE: WWW.MONGRELEMPIRE.ORG

This is a work of fiction.
All of the characters, organizations and events portrayed in this novel are either products of the author's imagination or are used fictionally.

This publisher is a proud member of

[clmp]

COUNCIL OF LITERARY MAGAZINES & PRESSES
w w w . c l m p . o r g

Book Design: Mongrel Empire Press using iWork Pages

This Book Is Dedicated To Deborah

I Promessi Sposi

"For Those of You Who Are Scoring the Game" and "Nolan in the Badger Café" were previously published in the online edition of "Oklahoma Writing" in *Sugar Mule* (M.L. Weber, ed.) and in the print version of the anthology entitled *Ain't Nobody That Can Sing Like Me: New Oklahoma Writing* (Mongrel Empire Press, 2010).

CONTENTS

THE INSUREDS

My travel log says it was the 12th of November, 1959, a Thursday afternoon. The leaves were thoroughly brown and going, the sky blue for the last time in twelve weeks. Susan and Armand sat before their old sweet-smelling gas heater, in a room full of linoleum which tried to creak with the pain of rich character when walked on, but lacked the refinement of tone permitted only to houses built with generations in mind. The spacing of the joists, the depth of the crawl spaces, the grade of the lumber, govern music as well as function.

I warmed my front, rubbed my cold back on the textured plaster wall. The electricity was turned off, so was the telephone, and the gas stove sounded desperate as if it was next. In the bathroom, to which I repaired needlessly to distract myself from Susan and Armand by looking into the monkey-faced mirror, I found green and red stains in the tub, copper and iron parodying the chromatics of Christmas yet to come.

They told me, laughing, that no one would anyhow bother to evict them. "None of this property hasn't any value to threaten," said Armand. He was only forty, spring-loaded and able, and I asked him why he didn't leave for other parts.

"I don't want to go down with the ship," he said. "Uh huh," I said, puzzled, waiting for some completing or explaining of his thought. But he was silent. I would later get it, dealing with him after they moved to Texas and Susan had died in their car within the 90-day, still Oklahoma covered. What he was saying was not answering why he wouldn't leave, it was agreeing and saying he would. Armand stripped everything down, like for a car race, left out the connectors.

"We'd be poor Oklahomans if we ran from thin to fat when trouble comes," said Susan. She didn't get Armand either. "Anyhow, we got your disaster insurance."

I looked at her. Her hair was trained into wisps, as if she was hoping to be mistaken for a whole pack's worth of burning cigarettes, and it was clearly hard for her to sit still, her eyes red as new blackberries, whereas Armand moved little but his lips.

"Act of God," said Armand, shaking his head at her.

"What?"

"Struck dumb. Plague of flies. Tornado. Like this is." He mimicked a vegetable, eyes blank, lips loose, then straightened. "There's a Ford out past your wheels, there, that won't go into reverse. The school ain't teaching Edwin anything, since he's 11 and can't read the bathroom door or count the apples on the teacher's desk. Your policy talks about Acts of God."

"So?"

"Can a Act of God be a lot of ordinary things that get together to wipe you out?"

I laughed. "Try to fly that iron bathtub to Europe," I said.

"It could be worse," said Armand. "We got eggs and okra and fresh salsify."

"Yeah and 12 bottles of Coke," Susan put in with a loud sigh of mock relief. Armand grinned and said, "You're the adjuster, tell me something."

"What's that?"

"What's the craziest claim you ever had?"

"That I ever paid, or including ones I denied laughing?"

"Either or neither."

"Well, you can always get a couple hundred out of me. We pay the lawyers that much for the paper cuts they get reading the claims we don't settle. I'm thinking of when the father of the firebug claimed $4000 for a dollar deck of cards when his barn burned down."

It was 1951 and just as blue and bright as today. People still kept dry corn cobs in the bathroom to strengthen your teeth, though if you ever looked at a pig's dentation, you would scratch your head in puzzlement at this custom.

Little Jock Hriska lived on a farm with his parents and four siblings, the two eldest being in the wheat fields on some winter-crop affair, and the babies being with their mom headed for the nearby town of Gritzburgh, at that moment dreaming of sucking horehound drops inside Sutcher's Trading Co.

Before the dust of the Studebaker was settled back into the potholes in the dirt road, the rampage was begun. Jock stripped naked and, gouging a giant glop of new butter from the ice-packed churn, he greased himself all up. He was a cow. The cow was stuck in the silo and had to be greased to get through the door. Having grossly overeaten within, she was the biggest heifer below Heaven, an achievement which suited Jock.

The cow was fed a few cookies from the jar atop the Home Comfort woodstove, as celebration for having gloriously and notoriously escaped. It felt so fine, in fact, that it had to be eaten for supper by a winning gambler named Joker Hriska (the whole beef, bones and all).

> If fat and fine
> On you they'll dine
> The thin and starved
> Are never carved
> —Sinbad

The same Joker Hriska who fortunately found in an elder brother's boot a limber deck of Aviator playing cards with which to calm the extreme satisfaction of his belly, filled as it was with cookie-steaks. Joker was lucky in cards every hand, taking a big jackpot of screws, bolts, nuts and washers (the four coin denominations) from a disgruntled phantasmal saloonkeeper woman named Adeline Gristle.

But Adeline was a dead ringer for Ma Hriska, so he tipped her a bolt and some screws and threw the rest of the stuff up over his head in wild joy so that it spilled all over the kitchen-saloon floor. A long famous Walter Huston laugh: fool's gold from the mother hill. She ran straight to town to buy French Lace curtains from Sutcher's with her tip. Jock could only pray Ma Hriska was not about to buy the last pair of French lace curtains. It would not be pretty to watch.

Having thoroughly debauched the innards of the homestead, Jock was mindful that the gambler Joker had left a wife in Topeka, at first forlorn but later grim. She had a little ax, and she had a box of matches that she kept to burn down saloons and other articles of the devil.

Well, she caught up with Joker just as he'd cleaned out ole "Alcohol" Woods for the third time in the pilot house of the steamboat "Margrit Jane." Alias the barn's loft, to which Jock, now Joker's vengeful spouse Emma Hriska, repaired with a Domino matchbox and his trusty rusty hatchet. And the fifty-two demons.

He hacked them and whacked them at every angle, like a drunken hibachi cook, splitting and binding the devils with imprecations fit more for a theater puppet than a Carrie Nation. Then he set heaps of shreds on fire.

It caught the hay beneath it and Jock fled to watch in terror as the structure burned, out of sight of the human world. And he felt the great blue bowl of sky, certain of its work as the haircut bowl but immensely grimmer, sealing him under it.

Jock forgot it on and off as the day went on and each time he thought of something new to say and each time the level of his terror lessened. When Ma Hriska got back with the twins Margaret and Jane, he was calm as a breeze. "What happened to the barn, Jocky?"

"Lightning has struck it, Ma!"

"Who has done this to our barn, Jocky?"

"I knew you didn't like big brother to play cards, Ma, so I took them playing cards from a boot and I went out to the barn and I prayed to Jesus to strike the tarts and pimps dead, AND HE DID!"

"Strike the WHAT!?!"

"Them Kings and Queens and Jacks, I heard Revival Preacher call 'em that, for rollin' the marks for their cash, and leavin' 'em with the dread disease of gamblin', so I guessed they must be some bad demons locked in."

Ma nodded her head; that was alright then. She sat in her big chrome campaign chair, the one the blue coated general used when he oversaw the removal of the heathen Pawnees to Osage country, and took her Jocky in her lap.

Well, when Mr. Hriska came in with the brothers, he didn't lift a finger against Jock, but he called me and said, "I want to make a claim."

He said his barn was burned and I asked him what it was worth, "It don't matter," he said.

"Well," I said.

"I ain't claimin' the barn."

"Well?"

"I'm claimin' the pack of Aviators."

"The pack of cards?"

"That's it."

"Below your deductible, don't you think?"

"Not a bit of it. Jock burnt the cards. Cards burnt the barn."

"The tarts and pimps?" Word had gotten around.

"Barn's worth thirteen, fourteen hundred. But the law says the barn burners pay triple for their rotten crime 'cause they meant to. Cards was evil. Jock had to burn the cards. No cards, no evidence, but the cards done it, all right. Getting away with it because they were burnt too. Aviator Company goes off scot-free. If I had 'em those cards was worth four thousand dollars to me."

"Jock's an angel," I said.

"Bet he is."

"You deserve the claim I'm sure, but you won't get it."

"Won't?"

"Act of God."

Susan and Armand laughed till tears rolled down their cheeks like clear marbles.

NOLAN IN THE BADGER CAFÉ

In the Badger Café are the usuals but as usual also some unusuals. In the circular booth in the corner are some bikers—not the greasy Outlaws with Sex Pistol knockoff names whose prodigious leather-mashed asses Nolan has kicked on several occasions—but untattooed doctors and lawyers and brokers in clean black leather, men and women. Their bikes are in clean formation out at the edge of the lot. They are considerate. A bit disappointing, really. They are thanking the waitress, tipping well.

"Fry some triple twins, Nolan?" asked Dee, her mountain of hair triple-clipped into a stout pile. He nodded, "Thanks, Dee." Two eggs and two strips of crisp bacon, two tomato slices on the side, no carbs. Nolan, who was polite to a fault, looked her in the eyes when he said it. Some found it attractive, some disconcerting, according to their characters and temperaments, that Nolan looked straight into their eyes when he talked. It was a bit weird at the least—there was no squint, no postured drollness, no twinkle, no expropriation of a straight look for some agenda of being impressive.

The truth was, directness came naturally to Nolan. The politeness did not; it was a learned safeguard against Nolan's propensity to straight talk. Some interpreted the directness as special to them, a powerfully seductive singling out—as if you were the Lone Bank of Love and he was about to rob it.

Others viewed it as an equally seductive indifference to them, a sign of great power and self-sufficiency: Nolan, the Loan Banker of Love—if you need it, you can't have it . . . .

Nolan sat down in the booth, reached into his black leather satchel, and pulled out his own handmade 365 day Thoughts Calendar. He turned to May 5, 2003 and read this entry:

Pig is the most shameless animal

The pig is the most shameless animal on the face of the earth. It is the only animal that invites its friends to have sex with its mate. In America, most people consume pork. Many times after dance parties, they have swapping of wives; i. e. many say "you sleep with my wife and I will sleep with your wife." If you eat pigs then you behave like pigs. We Indians look upon America to be very advanced and sophisticated. Whatever they do, we follow after a few years. According to an article in Island magazine, this practice of swapping wives has become common in the affluent circles of Bombay.

–Dr. Zakir Naik, East India,
President, Islamic Research Foundation

Dee appears with his eggs and bacon, sets it down. "Want my bacon?" Nolan asks.

She is used to seeing him with the book, expects the unexpected. Dee is studying for a math degree at the community college in Okmulgee. Smarter than Nolan may realize, she knows he's not a mere untouchable asymptote, only a little but infinite bit out of reach of her moving curves—or, he lives in negative territory on the other side of the asymptote, visible but not even close. He is older by a lot, for one, severely attractive but weird like the assassin from the future in Terminator II.

"No. I don't want your bacon. Don't you want it any more?"

"If I ate it and married you, according to Dr. Naik, I'd start wanting us to be swingers."

"So is that some sort of sidewinder proposal of marriage, you forgoing the bacon?"

"Just hypothesizing."

"I haven't noticed our customers getting more romantic after they eat the bacon."

"I wouldn't have thought you'd see swapping spouses as necessarily romantic."

"A shill-word for promiscuous. Pick at your breakfast if you want but don't pick at me. I'm not on your plate."

"Been out by Masada of late?" A closed rural Aryan conclave.

"I give it a wide berth."

"What do you hear?"

"They're still not gentlemen and ladies."

"That's freedom."

"Yeah." Nolan hears the cook ring the bell, say, "Dee Ann, please." She eases away to the pass-through. She is always polite with something in reserve, dry as a July creek bed. Nolan wonders if the cook says please when he is not there. Most of the rudeness he encounters is from the oblivious. There is something about Nolan that makes tutored men remember their manners; like the sense of a live power line unseen touching a pipe or rain gutter, you can hear the hum nearly, but you have to be deconstructing your focus to notice. Nolan knows this about himself, knows old Darwin's laws are at work there.

"Where is the *fucking* tabasco?" A deep voice with a very British accent somehow rises above the light roar of the diner. As he tightens, Nolan's vanishing Observer mind remarks that somehow a British voice even at its deepest wraps around a very high note which rises up above every other sound—a countertenor pig wrapped in a bass blanket. Listen to John Cleese sometimes. The inflection does wonders with sound!

Nolan is contra-verbal now. He stares at the source of the question, like a falcon on some invisible wrist. He is hooded by an intention concentrated with attention.

The speaker is graced with a shock of huge gray hair over a black boatneck T, massive arms forming an A with the table, palms together before his massive hairy chest with tips touching lightly in a mockery of delicacy. "I did ask for it minutes ago." Nolan rises, takes a three-quarters full tabasco from the counter to the man's table, where he sits with a very petite and rather shriveled redhead.

"I am Nolan. Helping your server, she's rather busy. And what brings you to the blasted wastes of Badgerburg, Mr. . . . ?"

"Roger Ray. Well if you truly care, it is a Greco-Roman exhibition on your local green."

"Gay sex on the golf course, Roger?"

Roger bursts up from the booth, his legs knocking the table against the redhead.

"This place will do as well!"

"Agreed," replies Nolan, suddenly seizing Roger's neck with his left arm, casually unscrewing the tabasco bottle with his right fingers, popping off the plastic dropper, prying open Roger's clinched teeth with his left fingers, and deftly depositing the entire McIlhenny contents into Roger's mouth. Roger is absolutely immobilized by something Nolan is managing to do to the front of Roger's neck with his knuckles. Nolan shuts his mouth again and somehow holds it shut with his right hand, even making Roger's jaws pretend to masticate. Roger's face is growing ever redder as he tries to sputter but cannot.

Some there suspect that Roger might be close to death. He cannot breathe. Dee begins to cry out. The cook reaches to call the police. Nolan suddenly slams him into his seat, opens his mouth, pours a whole glass of water into it, which Roger spits out all over the table and the redhead, then takes a package of saltines from a dish on the table, unwraps it, and shoves all four crackers into Roger's mouth.

"Keep eating crackers," he says. "It will gradually take out the fire." Seeing that Roger will live now, the cook moves his hand away from the phone. Nolan turns to the redhead.

"I am sorry if you were splattered or alarmed. I am certain you neither partake of nor approve of your companion's rudeness, which is what entitled him to know fully where the "fucking" tabasco was. My principle with rude people is to teach them to be careful what they ask for. It is unfortunate that you were forced to be such an intimate witness to Roger's correction." He turned to the restaurant as a whole. "Similar apologies to you all."

After paying matter-of-factly, Nolan nodded to wary Dee and the leery chef, and exited to his van. Through the diner's window he saw Roger ignoring his advice, still downing water ferociously. Definitely a new entry in the Enemy Book, he thinks. Nolan had found a thick, very old green journal book in a Hot Springs used bookstore and had bought it—no entries—for its resemblance to a magic book. He termed it his rutter—maritime jargon for a sort of logbook or guidebook of the ocean and its currents, harbors, pitfalls. In it he kept names, addresses, and anecdotes about people who might have reason to do him harm. A book of baddos.

He'd really meant to feel the pulse, not be the pulse, of old Badgerburg. Responding to rudeness was his Achilles heel. Nolan figured he had the sympathy of the café customers—however appalled they might have been at his lethal style of retort. He was however glad this was not really his own land.

CONFESSOR

I must tell you that I never thought anything would come of going to the confessional. Of course I was not one of the Catholics and did not know the rituals. I'd stayed clear of them pretty well, which wasn't hard since they'd get about five cars on Easter and one was the priest's. They'd recently become more tolerable on account of President Kennedy.

It all started with the calf that my wife Billie brought up to the house one evening, inexplicably sick. I was really scared of a quarantine, always had been even though that hardly ever happens to anyone. Every time a dog spit up on the grass I thought epidemic. Billie says I must have died in the black plague once.

The calf got well in a day or so, but she kept hanging around the back door. She wouldn't be run off to the herd, and I'm damned if I know how she kept breaking through the barbed wire—right along where I'd hung several coyote carcasses on the fence to scare off their friends. The fence wire was always busted through near the same posts, but she never had a cut on her little hide.

She was still supposed to be nursing, but all she ate was grass and she was getting thinner. Calf wouldn't nurse even when I roped her mama and tied them up together to the barn door.

It got to where she'd follow me everywhere, stand and wait at the egghouse or the garden gate. She'd kick at the coop door if she thought I was visiting too long with the hens. When I came out she would start licking at my ankles and calves if I let her keep it up. But who could stand that big old rough slab of tongue licking at you like you were the postage stamp on a box of chocolates for her boyfriend? Pretty quick I gave up my habit of slopping the hogs buck naked or in my BVDs. I'd pull on my overalls.

It got to be the joke for awhile, till the things started happening that weren't so damned funny. I waked up one morning and went out to get some eggs. Something had broke through and stomped seven hens to death on the coop floor and busted up most of the eggs. It sure wasn't a coyote or even a dog, nor a weasel or fox. Nothing had been eaten.

Two days later the heifer calf bit Billie right in her sitdown while she was hanging up her dresses to dry on the line. Then the calf grabbed one of the dresses in her teeth and tore out across the lawn with it, mooing ayoooo! Ayooooooh! Ayah ayah ayoooh, like nothing so much as a cow trying to sound like a coyote.

But the worst part of it was, the heifer brought the dress to me like she wanted to give it to me. But when I tried to get it she looked at me with her big reddened eyes and kicked me in the knee so hard it's never healed altogether, with her front hoof. Now they can't do that with the front hoof. So I thought. I fell down hollering and that heifer dropped one end of that dress in my face and worried it like a dog worries a bone. I was sick with pain, covered with July dust. Finally she mooed ayoooh and dropped the dress at my feet, picked it up with her nose and tossed it up onto her back, shook it off again, and looked at me.

"Hell," said Billie, "she wants you to put this dress on her. "Well, that surely was crazy, but I was as spooked as I was hurt. Those red eyes reminded me of something Billie didn't know and I wanted to forget. I couldn't stop thinking about it. I even dreamed about it and I never remember dreams.

"Breeze, breeze, I need a breeze," was what the calf kept saying in my dream. The voice sounded like it was amplified and I couldn't tell if it was male or female. Billie said I sounded like it wasn't me when I said "breeze" twice in my sleep.

So the next day I went over to see Julio Cortazar, this fellow from San Antonio I lease pasture from for my cutting horses. I asked him if he went to church up here and he said yes, there was a parish in Tishomingo and a young priest would come down to hold mass in Madill every Saturday morning. I asked if the priest was genial and he said very nice and grinned. I cannot figure what was funny, but Julio had this way of looking at you that made you think he knew what was funny and nothing else really was: kind of sober and amused. Not many of his kind seem very real to me, I'll admit.

Well I didn't want any part of a church service but I drove into Madill on Saturday afternoon on the excuse of checking out the sale barn crowd, but I went to the church on the chance I'd catch the priest. It was made of cinder blocks and looked like a mechanic's garage with its corrugated roof. The cross was a welded re-bar. But it was cool as the heart of a watermelon inside, and it turned out the priest was also a Hispanic fellow. English was better than mine. He was right at the little fountain up front when I opened the hollow core door.

"How may I help you?" Deep voice out of a teen looking face and thin frame.

"I ain't Catholic."

"Yes."

"I wonder if I can confess something, and if I do you still have to keep it confidential?"

"You must and I can." He put it backwards. At first I thought that was confused English. The Spanish put their adjectives after their nouns, too.

"Do we go to the booth?"

"No, we go to my office to converse."

We sat down in the tiny office at the back right of the church and while he rolled a smoke from a can of Bugler I told him what happened when I was 17 and lived on the other end of the state, up in the Osage. She was just a newborn and I was in a hurry and forgot to bring her and her mama into the nursery stall—they were both out there all night. The coyotes got her. One pup was kicked to death—mama must have fought hard. Dad never hung the coyote pup on the fence, but burned it, almost sorrowful. "It's not its fault," he said.

"Where I was, was down in the river bed with Annie Millen that night. No moon in the clouds. They used it then as a landfill, and the bulldozers had made it look like a desert: the river was always low and streamy so there were dunes and small pools of water everywhere.

"Annie pulled on her dress when we were done behind one of the dunes and got up to go wash in one of the pools. There were people all over that river bed, mostly naked, some with fires, and bikers were always roaring around the dunes so much you never much noticed them, just went on with your business.

"I was appreciating her, knees bent over the pool in the glow of the fires, when this cycle leaped over the dune in a cloud of sand and crushed her like a grape. She was dead in five minutes, never spoke. The rider who did it broke his leg, laid there so scared and crying so hard I couldn't be mad or help wondering at the fanged cobra-snake painted on his sleeveless leather vest, which was all he had on.

"Well, the next day, the doorbell rang and there was Annie's older sister at the door, holding an evening gown, the one Annie had picked out for the prom. When I opened the screen she threw the gown in my face, and told me she hoped I would enjoy it off her dead, since I took her out to the river bed to get her dress off her alive. She said God killed Annie so she could stop giving in to me just because she loved me.

"All I could think of for weeks was calf's eyes and Annie's eyes, and I moved down here away from there long after Dad and even Annie's sister had forgiven and forgotten. Annie's sister was tall as pampas grass and real slender, she's a Methodist bishop now, anyhow she even asked me to forgive her later.

"Well, I've never told Billie or anyone else much about any of this, in fact nothing. But I swear to you this calf knows something, and it's got me out of my wits."

The priest didn't act like I was crazy or try to talk me out of it. He didn't tell me to do Hail Marys or anything, either. He smiled and rolled another Bugler and talked quietly. I went home. Following his instructions, I took the dress of Billie's that the calf had rubbed in my face, a golden colored one, and I cut a swatch of it into thin short strips and then shredded them in the paper cutter in my farm office. Then I stirred it up in water with a little whisky and drank it all down. Every sip made me gag and it took me five minutes. The priest figured it would do for the prom dress, which I'd burnt up in the trash barrel those years ago, since the calf seemed to think so.

I went and got the calf and I took a hypodermic and filled it up with horse dope from my vet bag and I gave the heifer a big dose. The priest said not to scare her. When she went down for the Sleep I skinned her carefully and burnt her remains. Over the next few days I tanned the hide and had Ken at the boot shop make it into a vest and pair of gloves for me. I wear them every Sunday now, and Billie's not but I'm one of the Catholics. I do feel like those two spirits finally got untangled and went their separate ways—mainly away from me, for which I am grateful to God and my Confessor. Who says he will soon teach me how us Catholics talk to the coyotes, whose forgiveness I still lack.

GRANT SAYS NO

When U. S. Grant left office in 1876, he and his wife Julia went on a good-will tour around the world. It was good for him to leave the country at that time. His administration had been perforated by scandals due to Grant's tendency to take a man's word and a man's flattering words at their face value. A man who could read the character of the deepest southern generals and outsmart Lee was at the mercy of liars and braggarts when it came to picking trustworthy advisors. The good-will trip was his invention; it was designed as a curtain for his embarrassments. He was a man of strategy, not of intrigue and subterfuge. His value in politics, in short, was as a figurehead, and at least the good-will tour matched his value and capacities.

He was the most sincere and honest of men, as well as the most naive. Double-talk was a language he could neither comprehend nor articulate. When he was a teenager in Illinois, his father, a tanner, sent him to sell a horse. His father instructed him carefully, hoping to teach him the fundamentals of bargaining: Now you are to ask 27 dollars, and if he should offer 20, you are to say 25, and you may sell the horse as low as 23. When Grant appeared with the horse, he told the buyer, "My father says I am to ask 27, but may accept 23." You can guess what he sold the horse for. Grant would become the best horseman at West Point.

Eventually in 1878 Grant arrived in Japan. The social revolution there rivaled anything Grant had seen in the industrializing of America during his tenure. In 1867 the Meiji dynasty was restored to power, ending 264 years of rule by the Shogun and his samurai—longer than the U.S. has been a nation—and restoring to the emperor's throne a 14-year old named Mutsuhito (he became known as Meiji, the enlightened one). By 1878 the founding papers of a representative government were being drafted on a British model, and Grant would live to see the first parliament established.

Everyone in Japan was mad about Western culture. For the last 10 years western influences dominated a culture long kept frozen in Elizabethan era time by the isolationist Shoguns. Grant was swarmed with well-wishers.

It was spring, and the famous cherry blossoms were in bloom. He won the respect and love of his hosts instantly, because he was unfailingly polite and dignified. His hosts dressed in long-tailed suits and wore hats, as he did, and he felt quite at home. His cigars were a hit, and he distributed many to the officials and noblemen who clamored for his attention.

He was shown Japanese implements of war, from a tour of a swordmaker's smithy to exhibitions of throwing stars and Zen Archery. Grant was intense but silent as he saw a man hit a target 200 yards away with eyes blindfolded. Perhaps he knew, after the artillery-based carnage he had superintended, that such skill would prove as irrelevant as it was impressive: and would become a sport.

His hosts were at first at pains to seem pleased with Grant's natural reserve and taciturn nature, so counter to the brash sailor and tradesman qualities that they had come to associate with mass American character. His restraint created an excited but artificial stir which could not entirely conceal their disappointment in his passionless tact and politesse.

Julia and Ulysses witnessed a tea ceremony; Julia was ecstatic over its elegant precision and ritual, and he loved it for her sake, but there was a grim sadness in his heart which the ceremony could not disturb. He could not feel that its symbolism exceeded the intensity either of his love for his wife or of that same grim sadness occasioned by his brilliant perseverance in the War Between The States.

Always the shadow of Lincoln's death—stirred into fresh memory by the assassination while he was in Japan of Okubo Toshimichi, one of the founders of the new democratic wave, by old feudal rivals—cast itself over Grant as the tragedy of tragedies. He and Julia had declined Lincoln's invitation to join them at the Ford Theater that night—would his sentry's instincts have thwarted Booth?

Finally, his sensitive and anxious hosts resorted to the No Theater in desperation. With sensors finer than the antennae of the ant, they knew that this Ambassador of a culture whose ideals they had embraced had not been truly stirred. His visit was considered a gauge of future symbiosis between the two countries and cultures.

No was a centuries old form of imperial formal theater now limited to performances on the grounds of the emperor's palace in central Tokyo. It was so ritualized and abrupt that it ran against the new western craze. Every gesture, every pause, was scripted meticulously and rooted in 6 centuries of tradition. Variations were met with deep disapproval and disgust. Actors who failed in any detail had been granted hara kiri. The art form was dying.

The play was outdoors, on a sunken wooden stage; the audience watched from stone steps in a half moon around the stage. The plot depicted the war of an ancient king against ghosts who plagued the countryside, blighting rice, killing and eating horses. Starvation was everywhere. The king's oldest daughter was engaged to be wed to a neighboring warlord to placate him; he had been a constant gall and threat, and now unity was needed to fight the ghosts. But the King of the Ghosts had fallen in love with this princess and wanted her for himself. He would have no mercy until she broke her engagement and married him.

She was torn between two equally horrific suitors, when all she wished was to be in the company of her lady-in-waiting and read and compose literature.

The lady-in-waiting disguised herself as the princess, and deceived the ghost into accepting her. The pathos of her gestures—seduction infused with dread and revulsion—was considered the emotional climax of the play—the climax always came in the middle. The ghost drew out the spirit of the false princess; she was spirited away and the blight and raids ended. The princess sadly married the neighboring warlord; then the ghost of the lady-in-waiting sapped the warlord's strength so that he died. The princess lived on alone, with her memories and her communion with the departed spirit of her friend.

When the play ended, the General's escorts were astonished to see him riveted to his special cushioned chair, tears streaming freely, without shame or embarrassment. Julia was no less astonished than her hosts.

"What is it, sir?" she cried. He shook his head, and when he could at last find words, said: "This must be preserved."

Such was his influence, that the art was viewed in a revived light, which of course persists to this day in the modern No drama of Yukio Mishima, among others.

As for Grant: the shade of Lincoln lifted from his heart, and he went on at Mark Twain's urging to compose his memoirs, which were excellently written and sold well. But he would say that his proudest creation was a haiku poem he composed one afternoon after having been given translations of Buson (1716-1783) and an explication of how to compose them by the foreign minister—a form he found to reflect the simple form and complex content of a good military plan.

> Dead Lincoln's pension:
> Two cold coins over the eyes
> Which have borne interest.

And that is how Grant saved No theater from dying out.

FOR THOSE OF YOU WHO ARE SCORING THE GAME

Payday was cold, but there was enough March sun for practice between the afternoon clipper-clouds. The rest of the swing shift could be seen through the backstop, trudging up the hill from the plant past the company's billboard of the Milky Way hung on the chain-link right field fence. At the bottom the scriptural font proclaimed: "Frances Held Plutofuels. There'd be no Heavens without Held." The principle product: navigational fuels, or psychofuels, which were encoded to direct the vessels it thrust, obviating the need for navigational instruments and pilot control. The fuel could pre-program for predicted maneuvers needed to avoid astral rocks and space debris.

We were loosed a half hour early during the early season for practice.

Janet had just thrown me her first pitch, a slippery sinker which I took for a ball. As I waved my bat across the plate I saw Ace descending the far hill from the plant between his two bodyguards. He was carrying his bat like a Pluto rod, horizontally between two fingertips. It seemed like there was even some space between his fingertips. Electric Boy.

Once before, they'd pulled me from the plant floor to sit with Ace while he performed his computations. It settled him to have a woman sit with him while he worked, his pencil moving stiffly in chronically icy fingers at the end of his pipe cleaner arms. His head was no larger than my own diminutive skull, but rich with fine black hair like seaweed.

He favored Prince Valiant, which might explain how some of Held's more gauche shop-rats came up with jeering him as "Princess" or "Prince-ace." Now the bodyguard approached me, no shades, looking happy and nonchalant unlike any movie gangster's muscle, but she had plenty of real muscles under her Held t-shirt and cargo pants. She held out a note, folded into a tight triangle.

"What? Why?"

"It's from Frances. What are you doing later?" Hence the smile, the no shades, the flashing eyes.

"Headed to the family farm to harvest mountain oysters, dusk to dawn. Another time, perhaps." She winced and then laughed as she sat in the bleachers. "Better read the note now." The unfolded note, creased like a diamond, was terse:

"The boy insists he can play like a girl. This being so, teach this young bird to bunt."

I handed the note to Maria, who was serving as Ump. "How old is he?" she wondered. I told her about 19.

"Still hairless?"

"He's right in front of you for God's sakes." She looked me a "so what?" Maria was suspected of a salacious craving for males.

Innocence might surmise, "Frances thinks it won't hurt us if we stick him in batting ninth every few contests." Certainly he appeared to be starving for earth beneath his feet. It intoxicated him now: by the time he went through the gate in the backstop unaccompanied by his bodyguards, he was trying on a woman's stride. Which made Janet chuckle. "Helen," she said to me, "Batter up."

"Helen, where do I stand, left or right?" asked Ace in the clear counter-tenor of a Shakespeare song. I was surprised he remembered me—it had been two years since I'd incubated him during his calculations. "Right side, of course, you're a boy," I answered. He stepped to the left-handed side. This was not to be credited. A few heiferish men had made the league over the decades, but never a lefthander, on or off the field. Every hitter on our team batted left. "Stand on the other side, Ace, the left side is for righties. I know it's confusing." But he looked at me instead of complying. "I realize I can't," he said. "I have a cataract on my left eye."

"Does Frances know that?" He nodded. Does she remember it would be the better question. I looked around. Everyone else was looking at the darkening sky, either worried about not getting to hit, or finding something to look at other than Ace on the wrong side of the plate. Janet wound up, then threw one middling fast, with no wrinkles, and Ace lined it to right field, even with his back elbow pointed straight to the ground. Ruth barely made a shoestring catch in the right-field corner.

"You won't do that again in a million years," Janet said. The sinker's dip to the outside corner was as wicked as they get, but Ace picked it up like a kingfisher, lining what would be a clean double to left. He knew enough to run the bases, faster than I would have thought his pearly sticks could manage. Angel blew the throw and he wound up on third. Janet said, "I saw this sort of thing once in a girl from Ocracoke. His eye's in the end of his bat."

"Horrible form," I observed. We were talking like he was a dog, him standing right there. And I had been the one bitching at Maria for third-personing him in his presence.

"Form doesn't make a hoot," said Janet. You don't have to dance like iron filings to hold the magnet." This was over Maria's head; she was behind me leaning against the backstop, unconsciously pawing the ground like a bull, pouring on the pheromones; she went down to third base, making a big show of coaching, patting him on the back, rubbing his David Bowie shoulder blades.

In the locker room later he sat on his bench in his sweat shorts, biting his nails. Of course everyone but me stripped down as if he were a blind dog, never giving it a thought. I knew some polysexual era history and physiology, however, took anatomy at the Community College when I misthought myself a budding nurse. He was quivering. He turned beneath the pressure of my hands on his shoulders to straddle the bench facing me, his back to the room. White carbon eyes less pure than fervent. In every diamond dwells its burning coal.

"Let me look at your head," I said.

"It's not bad."

He couldn't catch, not even a floater. Ruth had brained him at second base with a pop-up. "Why the mosaic development, Ace?"

"I can't explain what it's like for me. Computation problems come at me, like meals through a slot three times a day, but piles each time. I get *mental* R&R, watch the ball team on TV, which is all I get with any blood in it."

Ruth slid over to lay a ginger compress on the knot on his skull, and Jan felt it tenderly. Elsewhere in the room wet towels were sailing and smacking flesh as if birds were lightheartedly being snatched by slobbering ocean dragons. It all could have been on TV, they sure cared nothing about Ace as audience even though he was the boss' son.

"Lately I've been fading in and out sometimes," Ace said. "Usually I can figure out what the next 8 pitches will be and what the next 14 hitters will do, down to whether the right fielder will have to dive for the catch, or by how many feet the throw to first will beat the third hitter. It's easy, it's laid out in my head like a chessboard in four dimensions, I don't need any paper. The game is absurdly simple. Still, when I'm not working on her computations, in my head I'm hitting baseballs all over the lot."

"You should go back into your head and catch those hits," I joked. Was I patronizing him like Maria? Ace looked at me and shrugged. "There's just my two eyes, a hardball, a wooden bat, vectors in a field of green sectors." So! He'd lied about the cataracts. He was a true lefty. If this were the Olympics it would be a chromosomal scandal.

This wasn't the Olympics, this was the plant's bottom line. Ace's unprecedented computational maturity accelerated production of intelligent plutofuels to one-third the time computers could program the fuel. This was money.

There are eraser songs that you sing to get nagging ones out of your head, the songs that stick like gum on the bottom of your mental shoe, eraser songs that don't themselves stick when they've done their job. The thrust of Frances' instruction lay in the bunt as erasure, I decided— bunting would purge his expensive echoing daydreams of line drives— there was her emphasis, not on fledging the "young bird." She did not EVER want him fledged. Well, Frances, this is why it's *your* company.

Ace was starting to calm down; I really *am* a woman.

Ruth had called down the photographer, a wispy blond named Daniella, who like Ace looked about 14. Ruth is the team captain for psychological warfare, or Razz. She had Ace stand like a white spider in the center of a circling web of naked sluggers two heads taller than him;

Ruth made him strip—over my objection that he would get too cold, which was the best thing I could think of without getting them suspicious of my motives. He would in fact get too cold, anyhow.

I knew what Ruth was after with this shot. Her previous sally—a shot of the team with an older man in an apron, trainer or master watchmaker —made the team seem a finely tooled, frozen juggernaut in icily peak condition. Historical inevitability. *So, isn't it simply and classically* **no contest?** was the liminal message that seemed to induce hypnotic languor in the opponents, who in theory are rendered secretly avid for their own annihilation by this photographic maneuver.

On the other hand women with a frail boy gives an impressive jolt of power, a shock. It ties you in as infrared blood-sisters, Minervas having burst out from his big cranium and thin thighs. Venuses all married to their lame genius Vulcan. Ruth had been to more than college. "Daniella," Ruth said as the etheric photographer packed up, "just caption it 'Ace Held, Rockets' new backup DH.'" The word backup was a sop to the now-nominal designated hitter, Maria, who struck out a lot.

It was daring, capturing the image of the owner's son to count coup on the competition, taking a huge risk in crossing Frances' purposes, but tough women like Ruth were one-woman unions. Which Frances knew as an ex-steward who had parlayed our dues into minority ownership to leverage her buyout, her own majority stake coming also from our skimmed dues, it was thought.

After the photograph with short story appeared on the net we received Frances' second note: it was a tone-deaf, "What did I ask you to teach Ace?"

Janet and I worked him. "You two are the cows, you do it," had growled Maria, the batting cage captain, sour over his cold-shoulder to her advances and beginning to see the light of her own flame-out as well. It was a matter of "breaking" a hardwood bat with a life of its own, same as breaking a horse. Janet threw changeups so slow they bobbed like apples in a damp breeze. Ace was mesmerized at first but the eye in the end of his bat soon got the idea; in one afternoon he was laying down unreachable rollers that tracked the inside of the foul lines like radar.

Every few hours the bodyguards delivered snatches of computations to the dugout. They took Ace about thirty minutes to perform. It was three days before Ace confided to me that each time they were the same computations; he was screwing up. The male in him was getting ever ghostlier.

Ace came up to me at the concessionaire's 20 minutes before the season opener with the Tomahawks, and ordered a turkey dog with dijon and pearl onions. We shared a burgundy cooler, standing very close, and I enjoyed his flower-scented cologne. His voice was creeping a bit lower, careful of its new alto buds. "Helen, Frances is pissed as hell," he said. The womanly strong mouth was a fresh twist of second-hand lemon, too. "She said she'd take my ascended orbs." The x-rays were looking more like ovaries every day, he added. "And you know she doesn't ever speak figuratively. I guess you can see from the problems getting kicked back that I'm losing the touch. She's augmenting me with those dusty computers even now. They didn't catch my first botch."

"What did that do?"

"2300 lives and a clipper to Io were translated into radio waves."

"Dead!?"

"More like life as a moebius strip. Looping."

"But how can fuel cause that?"

"What do you think happens when you refine close to absolute purity? Things disappear into thought. Apotheosis for the Io clipper on account of my daydreaming during fuel encoding calculations, or even because of subconscious events. The reverse of what's happening to *me*."

I started laughing silently. He took the cooler from me and drank. "You laugh like that when you're afraid," Ace observed. I wrung my dampened hands, then dried them cathartically on his red undershirt sleeve. It was hard to follow his description, but not to feel what he was feeling. "SO—what do you mean the reverse? What's happening to you?"

He looked at me and I could see the friction in his eyes. "She'll do anything to pull me out of the dive, even if I'd rather smash up." Suddenly he touched my breast. I slammed his hand off, blurted,

"Queer!" then laughed, but he didn't look hurt or surprised. Limpid reflection eyes, not even waiting, suiting a wolverine more than a boy.

"It will never work, Ace. Against nature."

"If it doesn't then I don't care. She can put me under the knife and save herself a fuels process operative device. Whichever happens at least my brains won't dissolve into male pea soup and land me in the seminal breeder pool." Sappho has a masculine *ending*?

We had a few minutes before Play Ball. We slid into our empty locker room, took the training table. He rippled like an eel against my delirious flat muscles, and I sensed the burgeoning caves within him.

When Ace stepped into the batter's box, her eyes were flashing. In high crystal tones she chanted some razz at their pitcher. The first pitch she bunted along the third base line, threading it barely fair and barely foul like a helix before it ended up dead in the fair territory dirt as she hit the bag with her foot. The Tomahawks never had a play.

I was coaching first. This new Ariel leaned over quickly and nibbled my ear. "Frances already has herself a new pigeon, Helen!" her voice going up high over a siren beyond the fence. "The transistor just said the *Io* clipper has landed thick as granite, all hands fit." The radio device glinted, silvery in her ear. A minute voice from its receiver crackled over strings and horns. She easily beat a pickoff throw back to the bag.

"Oh Helen," she predicted, indicating my flat belly with her index fingers, "she'll be a girl." She laughed. "Just like her Daddy!"

"I thought of a good name for her," I said.

"What?"

"Tiresias."

For our journeywork on the plutofuels floor, the law requires ovarial but not gonadic sterilization to guard against teratogenesis. For reproduction we have implants.

I admired Ace's brilliant (but now unsteady) gift of prescience—still do. But in that sort of thing you have to be careful of *projecting*, don't you?

WALNUT EYES

Minutes after my birth my closed eyes looked like walnuts, ripe with the silver nitrate they dropped into my eyes in case my mother had gonorrhea. Of course China, my mother, would have no such thing, but those were the halcyon days of empirical medicine, a scorched earth policy toward all microbes. I was the firstborn, should have been glad Herod's thugs weren't looking for me.

The blackboard of my memory didn't come with erasers. I remember absolutely everything, from the moment I was born. I still had a calm view into the cascade of lives which had plunged me into this newest pool of life, rolling away from me like the half-minimized screens in Windows Vista. In my most recent life I was a journalist in New York, dying young in '38. In the birth room I heard a doctor mention Harry Truman's stance toward the new Israeli state, and I knew who Truman was: a Senator from Missouri and why would he even have a view about a new Israeli state. But from deep experience in the Windows I knew that there were always gaps between lives that had to be filled in. It was the gaps that kept me reincarnating, the insatiable curiosity that kept unkilling this hepcat.

It turned out that Truman's support for an Israeli state was crucial, and the state emerged less than two months after my March 23 birth. I was sandwiched between Gandhi's assassination less than two months before my birth, and the apotheosis of Zionism. Since I was an Aries on the cusp of Pisces, I realized I would be a sort of muted warrior. The fish swam backward toward peace, the ram crashed through China's canal into wars.

My first past-life memory—actually accessed inside China's cavity— was of the news of the death of Lawrence of Arabia. In May 1935 he swerved his motorcycle to avoid two boys suddenly appearing past a dip in the dirt road, and crashed headfirst. Perhaps it came to me because exactly three years later I crashed to my death from a New York skyscraper, simultaneously with a wrongly loved peer named Scroop Amsteren, (a Dutch heritage blueblood) from a visibly adjacent skyscraper—thus avoiding the social trainwreck of the outing of we two boys by the sports editor at my paper, who'd literally vomited when surprising us in the W.C. As I plummeted, a life flashed before my eyes— this one now. Consequently as far as I know I am the rare bird afflicted with clairvoyant deja vu. This may not really be rare for real birds, who always know where they're going even on their maiden flights south.

I was at least safely away from the temptation of death's big apple, surfacing in Stillwater, Oklahoma. This was the first dispatch I filed with life's *Daily*:

How an Oklahoma Baby Ended the Chinese Revolution

I was born in Stillwater in March 1948. Since my mother was a little girl, everyone had called her China because her skin looked like porcelain.

My god-daddy Jack was a rancher who was beginning to prosper after he returned from the war.

When he saw me, he said, "Well, China, it looks better than my mangy old hogs!"

Outside the hospital room, this Chinese nurse overheard him, but she heard it like this:

"Well, China looks better than my strange gold dogs!"

She wasn't really a nurse, but a spy for the Red Chinese. She figured they had to be Fu Dogs. "Strange" meant the same as "foreign," didn't it? And everyone always talked about the oriental art Jack and China's mom brought back from San Francisco and the Pacific Theater!

So the Red Nurse got the idea to steal me and ransom me for the golden Fu Dogs. She'd sell them and send the proceeds to the Red Army, which already had old Chiang Kai Shek on the run. Gold into bullets! She was ruthless and stealthy! She very sweetly told my grandfather he had to leave, and told China that I was needed in the lab for a few tests. She bundled me in a blanket and whisked me right out of the hospital.

As ransom she demanded the Golden Fu Dogs. Of course there were no Fu dogs. Finally she exchanged me for $100 Grand which she wired to Mao's forces at Nanking, just as they were preparing to battle the Kuomintang forces.

So Mao purchased ammunition, and by the next year (1949) the People's Army had routed Chiang Kai Shek and sent him packing to Taiwan. She was a hero!

When I was 18 her face was all over the papers. I never forget a face. I wrote her in China, told her this tale: how I remembered everything even though I was a newborn because I was born to be a revolutionary, *and how I had:*

- instinctively subordinated my own selfish immature needs and desires to the cause of the revolution of the comrade proletariat against the corrupt capitalists of the Kuomintang, *and how I had*
- never once cried or asked for food which would divert scarce resources from the Red Army, *and how I had*
- never ratted her out even though I recognized her picture in all the papers.

She responded by having me named a Hero of the Republic and Vanguardsman of the Revolution. Who was she? She was none other than Jiang Qing, last wife of Mao Zedong—the one who became known as the ruthless White-Boned Demon.

Thus a newborn brought victory to Mao Zedong. Archetypes of Jesus certainly are pesky weeds in the gardens of doctrine.

* * *

Fitting topic, as my newspaper in '38 was the very rag Karl Marx had written for in 1851.

THE TERRIBLE BEAUTY OF ANGELS

In *The Spirit and the Flesh* by Walter Williams, an *alyha* is described as part shaman, part warrior, of ambiguous gender, often also filling the role of the wife of the chief. A European example was the Chevalier d'Eon of France, lawyer, minister plenipotentiary to the Court of Britain, Franco-Prussian war veteran, who adopted variously the dress of both genders, and fought duels by sword in woman's dress. Note: the Spanish termed *alyhas* derogatorily as *berdaches*—a slang word for homosexual prostitutes. Typically oblivious image in the colonizer's cracked mirror.

For the thousandth time the North American *alyha* asks himself why he left the bed of his chief and his wonderful warriors for jobs with such as these two lawmen, who can hunt but cannot seem to think for themselves. A Pretoria capitol man who does think at all, however, can turn on his friends like a blood weasel, witness these two. Now Tocomboi the judge is once again contending with Mandano the cultural attaché and conservator, this time over a woman.

They will not say or agree that it is because Lydia Crane is a good-looking woman. If Alyha says, "Set her free from the jail, and take her gifts," they will stamp the ground or look down at the ground and call Alyha crazy and stupid.

But while they argue over her sanity and her punishment, they are both staring at her picture, which is not even designed to inflame. Their taste is good. The ether burns out of her eyes. If they would *ask* to do what they want to do instead of doing what they *"must"* do . . .

You don't have to know thyself. Know what you want. Only ignorance of that invites evil. (Yet Alyha is first to admit not being best qualified to understand the peculiarities of exclusive love. What he doesn't consider is what her answer might be.)

Alyha has told them a lot, but not that Alyha's secret name for their special justice triumvirate is the Three Blind Mice. So intent on sniffing out—truth, facts, thrills. The three of them have been together for only a few days. But that is already a fair name.

Of course including himself as the third mouse is bemused and ironic. The government of the Midnight Boys in Capetown and Pretoria ranks them one, two, three: one the territorial judge for wisdom, two the conservator for truth and security, and three is Alyha, the spokesperson, for telepathy and voice of the accused. But Alyha is the only one of them who could also do the other two jobs.

The day is cold in Oklahoma City. The steps up to Tocomboi's lavish townhouse, top floor of the First Bank of Oklahoma in the middle ages, are slick with ice. Alyha constantly hears the wild white Bird people and their music, swarming and swooping in his ears, but the judge and conservator do not.

* * *

Cape Town remained capital for the parliament, Pretoria for Administration, and Mangaung (formerly Bloemfonstein) for the judiciary: Old South Africa's model.

"It is very, very sad," intoned Sana Sanganno, the planetary minister for provincial affairs. The day was warm for June in Cape Town, and the sky was full of opportunistic birds scoring fish and worms in thousands.

"Just heartbreaking," added Sanganno. "I am not very familiar with that musical people in Oklahoma, but the deluded frenzy of unaccustomed fieriness this woman has incited in them must be deprived of its fuel. The public health of the Turtle Bay province could be ramified adversely, coast to coast."

Mandano exhaled sarcastically, and both Sanganno and Justice Tocomboi turned to him with feline intensity, as to the rustle of a mouse along the wall. "Meaning?" demanded Sanganno in the resonant bass that had become both *de rigueur* and a cliche among Pretorian solons.

Mandano's voice was somewhat more tenor, betraying his unusually pure American Indian pedigree.

"Meaning that the musical brothers you mention are on a meteor trip that has surpassed the concept of hope. We are dealing with white *migration.* Too hot to sit still, and nowhere to stand."

You know, *instinct*, Mandano might have hinted. Hope and despair, they merge in a place called Hades. Where Lost Souls meet to eat.

"If you want to know their story, you have to feed them a little blood. It looks to me as if it will be their own, down the line," Mandano concluded.

Sanganno looked at Tocomboi. "Is this report the result of your Conservator's investigations?" Tocomboi made significant eyes at Mandano, then spoke:

"Please forgive my colleague, not the most stoic yet perhaps most epicurean of truth-elicitors among the ranks of Conservators. Mandano is a native of Oklahoma, and knows with his instincts perhaps what you and I, cultured in these green African houses like ancient Carthaginians, could hardly surmise about the modern Bird People of the Great Plains. I am certain that his wisdom rides behind his lyrical illusions."

But Tocomboi was plainly embarrassed. By association.

Sanganno struck an imperative, all-business stance. "You are both to leave at once for Oklahoma City, there to convene proceedings in the trial of this Lydia Crane. It is critical to prevent any further genetic as well as epidemic damage from the AIDS HIVe among the music-gypsy culture; it is critical that this woman's saintliness and alleged healings be investigated and debunked, and that she be judged for her own illicit promiscuities with individuals of the quarantined set of white males."

Mandano and Tocomboi recognized that Sanganno had first read what he was now repeating, and the style was classic ghostwritten Kenneth Kaunda, XVIII, perennial and hereditary president of the World Spectrum Coalition.

"Crane will be supplied an indigenous Spokesperson. Safe, expeditious journey, brothers. Oh, by the way. Many citizens are in terror, maintaining that the so-called Birds are cracking people's skulls open with mind powers. This mad rumor should also be laid to rest; we don't need any self-fulfilling voodoo to further cover these birdboys with esoteric mists."

* * *

From Alyha's diary:

Today in the cushion-car—isn't it a wonderful thing that while he asked me this, the judge was suspended on a powerful cushion of hot air —Tocomboi assumes the mantle of Socrates. He will make no assumptions at all. He will start from scratch. "Who are the Birds? Why are they called the Birds? What are their demands?" This is Socrates? Yet he would not imagine that I'd even know about Socrates. He thinks I'm sure that alyhas sniff fumes over cracks in earth and sneak around fucking each other all night in our little cells. But, ho! ho! I answered him, jolly as a telephone operator and as well-noticed.

The Birds, I said to the judge and Mandano, you hear them sing but you never come out of your house at night to look for them. There are words to their music, but you don't hear them. You think they are cries of hunger, or swooping to inspire terror or discomfort. Have you ever stopped one in the street to look at them? No. You don't have these birds in South Africa.

If I'd had naming rights as first spotter (and in a way I just might), maybe I'd term them Kervies, because Louis Kervran found out that carbon can change to silicon, or hydrogen to oxygen, in one beaker in the universe, and that beaker's a live body. The world within them, apprehended by any outsider's senses, will change the witness metaphysically and even metachemically.

Or Parker Jays, because Joseph Parker applied Kervran's alchemy to his own genes but could or would make only black males immune to AIDS and unable to transmit AIDS. Now we are all a bit black, except the white men in Turtle Bay Province. It's like glue to styrofoam, the immune factor won't stick to a white man's genes. It's the stubborn white male gene, but who knows why? Can't be isolated in the lab.

Who'd want white children any more than poison mushrooms, Judge? White men were given Homelands out here. President Jesse Louis Jackson, XII, Kaunda's ancestor, made it his first, reluctant decree.

We all laughed, blacks and browns and reds. White men gave us "homelands." Now we've got their lands and their gene-hungry wives, and we all sang, "Oh, Job, what bad things have you done?" and threw their Bibles of sick tales of fighting and raping into the trash.

The birdmen are kept in the Spectrum mercilessly. Odd law of the World Spectrum Coalition (euphemism for apartheid). Or is public safety the real reason? Curse of the Wandering Jew, as the wild prophets blare in their blogs? Music moguls' interest to perpetuate strange music to export along with indigenous hallucinogens? To sell Multinational Geographics?

Only now they've multiplied beyond the plan, enabled by potent accidents or mutations. While the Pretorian cat's away, they've paid white Pretorian women and sent the girls born back to the State, and for decades the illegal boys have flocked into the cities, and now they are the waiters and tickettakers and servants and housecleaners and foodhandlers. But what they listen to is not muzak. So now we rate a full judge.

Some are legal: sterile males only, bred in test tubes, then sent out to the reservations as babies to preserve the culture, and maintain the stream of endless mechanical efficiency—this efficiency not a raw but a refined commodity, like the wines of monks or the songs and counsel of eunuchs. Boy, those white unsexed hands are so nimble, those minds determined as ants and clever as mice. Endless genetic variations derived from one man's sperm. One man's! Who is this man? We don't know. The Birds are living tombs of the Unknown Parent. How few know that? Did you, Tocomboi or Mandano? One man, assuredly safe from contact with AIDS HIVes, found dying in an Ozark cave. Still frozen, in cryonic suspension. The billions of his spermatozoa still tapped.

Only now the boys are half cracked. Chemical breakdown? A sort of test-tube incest factor, magnifying traits? They hear different drummers. They're flocking. And we don't parley their lingo, do we, judge?

Once when the Red men were down under the white thumb, they fought back: "We talk, you listen." I hate to marvel at our engaging integrity and simplicity. The Birds say: "We talk, You Can't Listen."

They're thinking of tearing this place apart from the mind up. Speaking of which, Tocomboi, and you also, Mandano, I am not going to seduce you. Your poor systems can ill-stand such pleasure.

* * *

As the two Pretorians emerged from the gate, the Spokesperson, Alyha, took them by storm with a warm greeting of embraces, almost mock-Hawaiian in style. Mandano smelled strong sandalwood in Alyha's hair.

"You are welcome here, boys!" Boys? Mandano winced, looking a bit warily at Tocomboi. After all the generations, the little noun had retained its special tang for blacks. Alyha's inflection more reminded the nostalgic archivist in Mandano of an ancient gangster character. Good day boys, let's knock off Three Fingers Capellano. But it would certainly pass by Tocomboi this time, and not only because Alyha was so intensely redskinned and not white: a large teal-blue star edged in red paint blazed over Alyha's face as if lightning had struck it there. The teal was a hologram implant. And it swirled oceanically, suggesting auguries.

No softdata on customs Tocomboi had ingested—and Mandano had drenched him in reference disks—mentioned this, nor could have prepared him for it anyhow. The diesel-smoke face of the judge still betrayed no fear, but his eyes were perched like hawks on the ledges of their sockets, and he failed to speak return greeting to Alyha.

Mandano knew this high-tech makeup as the face of rarely seen Nangasohu, meaning Chasing Star. Nangasohu was a kachina—spirit of creative inventiveness who had landed on a meteor in the San Francisco Mountains south of Hopi Land, conferring mysterious gifts on that nation's adepts from the unused mind's dark continent. Who could say why he'd come?

The figure of Nangasohu occupied the lower corner of a mural painted on a courtroom wall in the Oklahoma County courthouse. Two hundred years ago, a painter from the Four Corners had painted it over a crass composite mural filled with covered wagons and oil derricks and white faces of corrupt governors in stylized insets. Mandano had read the catalog index of this newer fresco over and over, having had little else to do in a thousand preliminary hearings during the first years of his career when he was stationed in his hometown.

But all Mandano said was, "You from come from Arizona?"

"Who doesn't, man, who doesn't?" burbled Alyha in his disconcerting unisex alto.

Alyha was taller than he looked, because under his smooth red skin he was wide and thick; dinosaur-haunched. There were a few lines in his face; probably 35-45. Very thick lips, very big teeth in perfect shape and line—a big grin had never left it, which Mandano wondered at. Make a grin yourself, he imagined, bang your teeth against his like two rams clashing horns, see if they're solid or magic.

Oklahoma City was not merely second nature to Mandano, he realized as they skirted six feet over Meridian Avenue in their cushion-air limousine made of pure ultra-tempered Santa Fe glass. Oklahoma City *was* his second nature. Like the *nagual* of "San" Carlos Castaneda, the provincial metropolis welled up within him, wild with tentacles of ectoplasmic light and pure probing. The city swam, giddy and drunk with probing *him*, through the canal streets of Mandano's blood, much more than memory or the enthusiasm of past familiarities so crushingly dull to anyone else in company with any returning native.

Was this warmblooded familiarity why he could look into Alyha's drastic face without cold vertigo?

They took 240 to the Agnew-Villa exit, and soon were passing the old stockyards, the Cattlemen's Cafe and the cowboy stores still operating. Everywhere were black tourists and the red Five-Tribes ranchers in town to sell their spring cull heifers and steers. Flophouses and church missions alternated with lowslung hotels and licensed, elegant houses of poker and sex, all of the older, merely electro-hardened, Las Cruces glass. Darkbodied sex as usual on view in half the windows in the broad daylight; somehow exhibiting still excited the copulators, though certainly unremarkable to anyone sober in the street. But even before the missions, none of the drying-out bums were white. Nor had he seen a woman. Still keeping up standards, mused Mandano.

Alyha was looking down carefully, but still grinning, as if he were the inspecting god who'd made all that life down in Exchange Street and was finding it just copasetic. There were gems, stones, bracelets, amulets all over him, as well as a shirt pocket full of ink pens of all shapes, including several bent chiropractor specimens—for Alyha wore a jean skirt and a navy surplus shirt above leather sandals. His left fist was painted white and his right yellow—only on their backs. Cheyenne, thought Mandano. But he didn't know for sure.

"Twilight is my loveliest time of day! I forget all the troubles we're having," gushed Alyha with a large alto sigh, and Mandano was certain then that he was a council-alyha. No citizen brave would be so rudely indiscreet as to suggest himself as wise enough to detect trouble. He'd have to tell Tocomboi this.

Tocomboi quietly jammed himself against Mandano in the back seat, though there was room to the judge's left. Mandano visualized his colleague's flat black muscles as a pride of mother lions ready to spring away from branches, say, to flee from a poacher's cushion-car.

"Boola Boola!" Mandano stage-whispered suddenly, poking Tocomboi's ribs lightly. Tocomboi flinched, then forced iron control over his simplistic homophobia. Mandano laughed deeply.

"Hide your thoughts in a school of minnows, but the Spokes-bogey is a catfish," Mandano mumbled melodramatically. "If you go noodling, you may lose your noodle." Still you could hear Tocomboi's mind roiling with threatened equations: berdache, transvestite, queer, mocker, slug, etc.

"Shut up, Mandano," signed Tocomboi angrily with gritted teeth and clinched face, and Mandano grinned silently. Tocomboi made no connection between catfish and noodling; how could he, not an Oklahoman?

Alyha maintained casual dignity and did not look over, only out the window, but only Tocomboi imagined that his revulsed thoughts were not tangible in the car.

Tocomboi decided to seize the reins. Mandano didn't care for him to do this when he was uneasy. "Personally we cannot challenge your hospitality, Mr. Alyha."

"Oh, Oh, merely Alyha! it is not my name, but simply a handle. As you know, we Spokes give up our names and honorifics. We just have none. Perhaps this is so that there will be no name that *can* be besmirched, and so the main motive to become corrupt is removed! Ha! Ha!"

"But," Tocomboi said, "why are you not camped vigilantly by the side of your charge, Lydia Crane?" Mandano winced in alarm. Ask a samurai why his sword isn't drawn, and you might be speaking with forked body.

Alyha's voice went cold as snow peaks: "What did you say? What did you say?' He was suddenly furious as beating wings, and hawk-shrill. Tocomboi cringed in irresistible reflex. A mountain would have fled.

One would have thought Tocomboi had been caught stealing into a burial ground to eat corpses during winter famine. Alyha's nose appeared to hook and his eyes to sit back piercing from far deeper in his face; the turquoise star practically vanished in terms of its prominence. Indignation at Tocomboi's invasion of his province was hardly descriptive of Alyha's transformation.

"I believe you," Mandano said spontaneously.

The moment hung fragilely, then suddenly Alyha reverted, resuming his grin as he said, "Forgive me, I'm cranky from worry about the white Birds. In answer, Justice: because she is clear to me, like a still pond, cold with a coming storm. Vigilance toward Lydia lies in the truest clarity, Sir." Tocomboi was clueless, yet remained prudently silent this time.

Sure, just a standard Grump, thought Mandano. Alyha began to designate various skyscrapers by name and function.

"United Founders," he said. "Old White lookout and site of famous corporate festivals. The restaurant still revolves for a vast view."

"Let's get to the court," Tocomboi briskly ordered the driver, who seemed to have slowed up for Alyha's exposition. "Holy Dog," Mandano heard the judge mutter under his breath.

* * *

Tocomboi looked around the crowd, applying his skill of freezing or quieting a scene in motion in his mind. He made a habit of installing the mandatory silence in his mind before requiring it of the audience. This made the silence able to jell when his bailiff should announce it.

But first the defendant was produced before him, and the case called. "Adam Purgeon." Tocomboi groaned ceremonially, showing ritual reluctance to take judgment power over each defendant personally. "Purgeon, there is only one crime we can call you for. Why are you seen in these hills, breaking quarantine?"

Purgeon knew it was not time to answer, because his masked spokesperson—the *alyha*—was silent. The *alyha* was a psychic, supposed to speak the truth in Purgeon's heart, from the space where people do not truly conflict. Purgeon's own words would be heard later, but would be regarded merely as specially admissible hearsay. He had no idea who the *alyha* was. No more did Tocomboi, or any other there. These officials traveled from court circuit to circuit, also giving private readings, finding corpses, weapons, lost rings (but never the long-lost living—who might prefer to remain lost.)

Tocomboi's bailiff took a nod from Tocomboi and said, "Let there be enough quiet to hear Adam Purgeon's heart beating." And there was total silence, enhanced by the judicial sonic device which subtly excluded birdsongs, insect whirs, mammal growls from a wide perimeter beyond the stump.

Bongoists began to pick up the very beat of Purgeon's heart after Adam had stood for three minutes with all eyes on him. This went on for three more minutes, then stopped with a half beat, a skip, and then a full beat. Purgeon was suitably entranced. Tocomboi would take his evidence.

The first witness, an old man wearing black shirt and pants with canary yellow tennis shoes of the best make—the uniform of the Neighborhood Community Watch—stood up to ask and state. Tocomboi appreciated his smooth, sharp-chinned face, black as 3 a.m. and symmetrically carved with long dimples in his cheeks like cirrus clouds high and deep as the full moon in a 3 a.m. sky.

"Purgeon, you are white and a man. I found you in a barn, holding the wrists of a frightened white girl. Were you going to rape her or take her to get yourself children?"

If he'd actually done it, she'd have to be sterilized and aborted if pregnant, and then go with him to quarantine. This might win the goal of political suppression of her growing influence, but infuriate her followers who would never believe the charges were not trumped up.

If he'd kissed her on a cut, or her mouth had contacted a cut on his body, a particle of his humors, deadly as plutonium, could spread it. This was lose-lose.

The *alyha* breathed deeply and spoke, a woman's deep alto voice: "I could not have harmed her. I am not infected." The girl in question, Lydia Crane, suddenly screamed with joy and danced around the edge of the circle, bowing to the *alyha* every few steps in rhythm to some drums beaten by her vastly relieved brothers. The Cranes were Acadian.

Tocomboi breathed out. In suspicion, insulated non-black families often chose risks of incest over risks of AIDS hitting their males. Lydia's value as well as her happiness was preserved, though the Field Nurse Corps would still triple test her over the next three years to make sure. *Alyha*s seldom erred, however.

Tocomboi said: "Lydia!" and some blacks in the audience, which was all black but for the Cranes and Purgeon, took frowning exception to the joy in his voice and to the over familiarity of using only her first name: white could never be that right. "Lydia! You must still ask your question." His judicial weakness lay in relying on his own character hunches. A sucker for it. This girl was too immature to channel any revolt.

Lydia spoke woodenly, resenting that Adam was almost off the hook: "Adam Purgeon, did you know what your heart has spoken when you tried to take me?"

The *alyha* paused only one second: "I did not know if I was infected." Tocomboi struck quickly: "You are nonetheless free, Adam Purgeon. Return to your reservation. Court over." That was it. The crowd had to run at once, without a second's pause, when he spoke those words. They had to scatter a hundred yards away. This was the

Stump Law Act designed by Justice Parker to preserve respect for judicial authority.

But back in the condos, back in the mansions neat as museums where the strongest citizens all lived with their complicated sexual arrangements and interracial extended families full of half-siblings and third cousins, back where everyone's color would be richly varied into the subtleties of taupe, beige, umber but never light pink: there would be fury.

Another judge would have had Purgeon euthanized without question. To be freed was seen as a vile insult to Lydia Crane, as Tocomboi intended.

Mandano was furiously astounded at being bypassed. Her contingent had been empowered, not neutralized, united and belligerent. Tocomboi had harpooned a whale's canker without handling Lydia Crane in the least.

It was not only blood that was wanted; it was the lust of ghosts for death. Best feed them. But it was the *alyha* who struck with his meteor gaze alone, as his tenorous voice thundered "Woodenhead!" The judge's head exploded like a coconut grenade.

The rumors of such events were less than half true as to their source, but true enough, thought Mandano as he bowed and accorded Alyha his reverence.

The empire fell back in a thousand other such theaters.

THE PERSONAL

Wanted to fall in with the right guy kind so located Personals in the *Gazette*. Three weeks old, but still . . . it's the *Gazette*, they persevere, all Brie and Camembert, no American, they linger on the tongue, taste and be tasted. No whiz or velveeta. Not even with rotel.

> DWSM, DDF, wear condom while reading, never impregnated by ideas, compassionate, tender but spare and clean, hard driving ambiance like taking long walks through abandoned industrial detritus, read Kiplinger's in jazzcuzzi, eating starfruit and smearing its juice on lens of home telescope to study effect on Orion (it changed sex). ISO D/S/F or MtF TS, B/NA/HIS/ W, Str8 or Bi, for SWS, with melon breasts unbloated with silicon of infused capital, lips thin from dialectical kisses, knees bony from strategic groin strikes, skin pale from studying war no more but deconstruction. Hate travel, pets, New York Times Sundays or other damned days. Liars OK.

I'm leaving out #, get off it, saw him first.

Called, Hi, called from Gazette. "Coltrane to Danforth, west to Bryant, north to Covell, west to Santa Fe, north to Waterloo, east to Boulevard, south to 2nd, north to Guthrie. Stairway to Heaven." Which was how it traced on the map. "Make sure you're alone. Shake any tails." He knew I would map! Oh God. This is it!

How he knew? The sound of my voice? Or else he thought he would copycat Brando in *Last Tango in Paris*, figuring I'm too young to be the Bertolucci addict I've been right through *Stealing Beauty*. Big problem: lie about what? I don't lie, ever. What might I fuck up and say that he would believe to be a lie? So on my way up the teasingly indirect route he charted (Atlas Foreplay, one-handed so he won't drop the infant planet) I kept eyes peeled for semaphores, psychic clues revealed in leaf shadows crushed into the asphalt by the brilliant though gibbous moon in southeast quadrant. Texted him: **saw shapes change but no roadkill.** The spell was on.

He calls. "So, what?" he says, voice like a distant Harley.

"I am a razor slit, anorexic via bulimic via hedonistic, nymph driven." Not entirely none of the above, pick the truth.

"Just don't get lost," he said, and rang off.

Visualized a *Malaise Gloriosus* with crumpled intellectual fatigues, gold-rims, glaring coldly at the wan little moons drifting in and out of orbit about him, shrill gnat moons cursing his weak force and absence of gravity or anti-gravity. Strung-out theory.

I pulled into Guthrie, found the house on one of the extravagantly broad avenues near the enormous Masonic Temple, and parked Old Saab, hail pocked but polished, beneath a sycamore. I wished that I could impress him with strategic practical expertise in knowing birds never poop from sycamore branches. Like the hat thrown on the bed they see it as bad cess. He would see me in the surface of the Saab and it would confirm his choice. The purity within the non-pristine.

I am not into submission, make no mistake, just dreaming that his detailed yet obscure ad cloaked a Cupid ready to steer into the dark of my psyche, eat me alive, disappear before dawn. I wanted to feel him, not see him, in fact wondered if I could just burst through his door, cut the light switch and mash his eyes shut, squint mine hard, crash through furniture too dumb to get out of our way till we hit some horizontal, bed, couch, or, hell, floor.

Sure, I know there's not much raw stuff left to make a god out of, but the trick of angels is they make use of the materials at hand. It has to be tricked out, like a turtle's head or an oyster's pearl. But instead of following the *Last Tango* script, the stripped down model with no cupholders or cruise control, I just went up on the porch and knocked on the door and he opened it. I had let myself see him as young and lean and there he was, John of Gaunt, six-six if an inch, weight ten stone, Ichabod Crane.

"When did you last see the Headless Horseman?" I asked. "I, Salome, have brought him his head." He did not laugh. There was no light on in the house behind him. He had been sitting in the dark.

He licked his thumb and held it out the screen door to catch a breeze. "I think he will not come tonight. He needs an east wind, and they're scarce here. You had better give *me* the head," he added, and seized my hair and pulled me through into the dark entry. The screen door slammed. He kissed me and I knew the feel of mercury outside the thermometer but still standing formed and tall. His limbs were cables. I never thought to have the chance to make it with a suspension bridge. I did roar across it. It did sway so slightly. It did take me high above the bay. I did see the golden gate. I did just catch the prison island from the corner of my eye.

ZORRO AND THE IRON QUEEN

Roadmap eyes; vienna sausages heated on the radiator of a vintage car; licking money to get the cocaine. These are some of my favorite things.

—Maria Von Andros, Artist

You've got to be very careful if you don't know where you are going because you might not get there.

—Yogi Berra

Banks used to be rich-looking and beautiful, as if those two qualities were distinct from one another. They had color and texture, frozen in time at the peak of neoclassical opulence.

This one was tall-ceilinged as well, but a study in subtly intimidating neutrals. A covert uneasiness radiated by a decor ostensibly designed not to offend any taste, an artistic anti-choice, purporting falsely to omit all but bare function yet sprinkled with objects of no apparent meaning— e.g., a soffit emerging from the central load-bearing wall at mid-body height, proceeding for four feet, with a bunch of river rocks scattered along it in gray and black tones. Zoan dubbed the style Electro-Cute.

Real riches transcend and subvert beauty, reflecting the banality of zero-passion wealth, characterizing a faceless and unattainably complex elite with no live characteristics at all. Magritte's bowler-hatted wizard. We have no eyes other than security cameras into the past, but most likely you are really short, bald, and unsexed.

Zoan grew tired of these reflections. What would it be like to see without interpreting—just to see?

Television snow. One must sort mush. But I can keep figure and ground discrimination to a better minimum than this. Bridge over seawater (Merleau-Ponty).

The right door of the bank crashed open and the robbers entered. Most drove forward into the bank but the point man stuck his grease gun in Bill Zoan's face. In the space of three seconds Bill whipped the gun from the robber's hands, shoved its butt into the man's L'Eggo'd chin and nose, threw the gun into the glass door, kneed him in the groin, gouged both eyes with rigid digits bent slightly at prime knuckle, and smashed his ears with the heels of his hand. Bill Zoan then left the bank and went down the street with no word or gesture to anyone to indicate a robbery was occurring.

With any luck no camera caught him hammering the hapless bandit. He'd never left a trace of himself in any records anywhere and did not wish to start now.

He heard a rapid automatic burst from inside the bank, some screams, no sirens. He felt his back pocket for his wallet. Empty.

The man he'd beaten had managed to pick his pocket while he was getting pulverized. Bill Zoan grinned a sour grin. Grudging respect, he said to himself as he pivoted and ran the fifty yards back to the bank. Nicknamed the robber Sticky. Sticky and the Stick-up. Haw haw haw said the Crow.

There was a male crow always in Bill Zoan's mind. A constant commentator. This crow was not Bill Zoan. It was not a facet, a figment, a splintered schizo, a dissociative persona. It was a real crow and it fed on its own corn, he thought. Haw haw haw. The crow was not Bill Zoan's friend or confidant and did not care one whit about what happened to Bill. I have a beak, not a Bill, the crow said. Haw, haw, haw. The crow also had no name. There's proof it was not part of Bill Zoan. Within my world but not of it, mused Bill often. What a guru.

Its culture was suburban leisure suit honky. Rule out any 'hood emblem or symbol here, no doubt.

Bill Zoan re-entered the Copperhead Third State Bank and there was Sticky, groaning on his left side, bleeding a bit from his right ear, wallet not visible. Seven or eight customers were spread face down on the floor. Over by the tellers were the other two gun-wielders. Neither saw him as he used his foot to shift Sticky a few feet. No wallet. Bill Zoan knelt, withdrew his Swiss Army knife from his jeans pocket, opened the pair of pliers, and whispered into the blood of the ear: "Have you read *Berenice* by Edgar Allan Poe? But I wax rhetorical. I will extract your teeth with these miniature pliers if you do not indicate where my wallet is."

Sticky's right index finger (nail very dirty, Bill Zoan observed) pointed to one of the gunmen. Gross! Bill Zoan retracted the pliers and opened the nail file. With light-speed and deftness he cleaned Sticky's five exposed nails. "I'll catch your other hand momentarily," he promised, still in a whisper.

Bill turned his attention to the gunmen who still did not see him. He saw now that they had shot a middle-aged woman, a teller. Her body was slumped over the counter, her bare left arm bleeding but only venously. Other tellers were bringing forest green bags of money, eco-tote bags, to the taller Sticky-designated gunman who seemed most authoritative, brandishing a Glock. He was also L'Eggo'd. He was giving orders in a pirate brogue as a voice distortion technique. Bill pegged him provisionally as Captain Morgan.

The other gun-wielder (another grease-gun) never saw what blacked her out as Bill Zoan rammed her head onto the counter. Blood from the wounded teller smeared this gunwoman's bare cheek. She alone had no hose mask. Bill Zoan caught her grease-gun. Captain Morgan whirled in surprise, but Bill was on him too quickly for meaningful dialogue, seizing Morgan's hosed nose in his teeth and biting the end of it off, knocking the Glock from his hand, and jamming the woman's grease-gun into his left ear. Bill Zoan spit-propelled the nose-end to the floor as Captain Morgan shrieked.

"And as for Cartilage, it must be destroyed." That was not the Crow. Bill Zoan called this authoritative, faintly Britannic inner voice "Cato."

"My wallet, if you would," said Bill Zoan to Captain Morgan. "I see it in the tote bag. Please extract it for me now. Mind your ear." The grease-gun remained hard thrust into the corsair's ear. The Captain retrieved the wallet, now sobbing and shaking, and Bill Zoan hammered his temple once with the butt of the grease-gun, mercifully assuaging his pain and decommissioning him. He checked his wallet; all was there. "I need the manager," he advised the other teller. Despite her wounded colleague's crisis this woman was well together. "That would be me," she said. "Maria Von Andros. We were short-handed. May I call 911 first?"

She wondered at herself feeling compelled to explain why Her Augustness was acting as teller.

Bill Zoan ordered the customers to stay down and not look at him, then quickly moved to the wounded woman and checked her. "No 911 yet. If at all. These wounds are minor," he said. "She must have fainted. I need your surveillance tapes. I promise to return them tomorrow, with only my face redacted. There are no loose ends here," he observed with a wry expression. Sticky was still immobilized, the female robber still out, and the Captain was now spread-eagled face down, a position he had submissively chosen. He followed her to the back office near the vault, retrieved the tape.

Bill handed the Manager the Glock, parked the grease-guns behind the counter. There was an ink pad for thumbprints on the counter. Bill opened the pad, pressed his left thumb into it, and left an impression on the faux-marble counter.

"So they can know it was me, the Un-Perpetrator, as distinguished from *Ces Trois Mousquetaires ici*. And not an uncaptured co-perp. They will not be able to ID me because my prints are not on file anywhere. I can live with their description of me."

Sirens. She had pressed the call button. No time to clean the other five nails. "Sorry, Sticky," Bill said as he passed the robber. "No nails symmetry. Mind your cuticles."

"I am not a hero," he said to the manager. "I promise." Bill Zoan loped gracefully from the bank and was gone.

He did not return the surveillance tape. Just say no to bad architecture. But the construction of her face . . . .

* * *

She'd wanted an anchorage to channel her as she wrote and painted, and there was Copperhead. A cover. A disguise. A magic cloak. She had wanted what the hero now showed her could be had. Therefore she was very vague with the sketch artist. When the detective accompanying the sketch artist became impatient, she was crisp in return:

"It was my first bank robbery, officer. I promise next time to set the safety of my customers at a lower premium than your needs for accurate likeness of the heroic intervenor. In any event, why must you find him?"

"He is under investigation for using excessive force against Mr. Craighead." Mr. Craighead was Sticky.

"Ah, the Batman offense."

"What?"

"You unwittingly make the case for vigilantism as an unintended consequence of your arguably jealous pursuit of the heroic Samaritan. You appear mean-spirited. I am a liberal, but our savior had a gun at his throat when he rearranged Mr. Craighead's anatomy."

"What?"

She gave up. "This is the description I have to give you.

She could draw it herself, of course. The mouth, forehead, eyes stood out in the wine-dark background of her imagining eye like Cheshire Cat body parts. The eyes were an amazing changeable green that contained all the colors– white, move over. Nothing in the least sinister; nothing in the least romantic; yet somehow electrified and full of brilliance. His ears were perfectly proportioned with attached lobe, intricate cartilage, hairless. Eyebrows thick and yet neither dark nor light brown. Moderate beard on his shaven face, close haircut like Trajan's statue. But it was part III of Hadrian's late-life poem which recurred to her from her university Latin course:

> Animula, vagula, blandula
> Hospes comesque corporis
> Quae nunc abibis in loca
> Pallidula, rigida, nudula,
> Nec, ut soles, dabis iocos.
> [Tight spirit, vagabond, irresistible,
> stranger and guest of the body,
> now unleashed in places

Pale, stringent and barren,
No more jokes, now you're alone?]

She had painted Trajan and Hadrian together from the Wikipedia statute images, the faux father and faux son, so accomplished and opposite, the interface where their hands clasped one another's right forearms, their looks steady into the other's eyes, but Trajan's half was a Roman forest full of wolves and wolves' eyes, Hadrian's half was a Greek forest full of satyrs and nymphs and fountains with the Nile River flowing through it. Trajan straight, Hadrian gay but sad, the Patras bust of the young Antinöus floating face up in the Nile behind him like Ophelia; yet in the penumbra of convergence of their two worlds, central to and in the tableaux, the power of order was met by the power of aesthesis at least halfway.

The painting was magnetic but did not sell because it lacked whimsy –well, it was too precise, too on target for escape from it to be possible, and people often bought art for escape. I mean, where would you hang something so huge and unsettling? Well, it was for herself. She could paint other things well that would not provoke such fears. What bothered her was him. Zorro, she provisionally dubbed him. He brought Hadrian and Trajan together, it hit her between the eyes, without a gay bone in his body. She would have to keep him, and that insight, to herself. Her gay friends would be pissed if she shared what she knew. Even the bright margin-dwellers live in lockstep.

* * *

A month later. Zoan is looking for a pair of pliers on the Avenue of the Americas. Ha.

So he tries the east-west number streets, still well-north of the diamond district. And there he is – behind bars.

No one has dared seize him physically; so no one to fight. His prison is canvas, glass and iron, in layers: a barred store window. The painting is the only thing in it, on a brass easel. Someone has captured him so precisely that it could have been a mirror– but that was reflection, not perception. The painting was framed in some bluish steel, the background was pewter pocked with dings as if pelted with meteor pellets, and then his face, precisely rendered as no photograph can do.

The signature: Korē. Zoan googled it on his phone: in Greek it means young maiden and refers to the unnamable queen of the dead. So he stands there scanning for clues when he sees it in the lower right pewtered corner: a faint yet distinct streak of copper paint. Her face flies into his mind like a winged bas-relief, from the bank. The Iron Queen.

There is no percentage in waiting. It's back to the bank and to the face that has floated through his mind a thousand times. Devil take his mask.

WHIRLWIND ROMANCE

Cortni Justice had once loathed the cutesy spelling of her given name. What were they thinking? That she would remain an infant or toddler well into her forties? She didn't even care for the standard version of her name—Courtney—being something of a traditionalist—in fact her father called her Miss New Zealand—more British than the British, more queenly than the Queen.

Along about age 14 she had taken to shortening her name to Cort, of course inspiring her equally precocious peers to ask if her middle name was "Of,"—"Cort of Justice"—and where were her columns, her bench and gavel? It was true: Cortni was very much the fact-finder and the renderer of judgments, though she did not make her judgments especially harsh.

Now, as she guided her Lincoln Navigator gingerly into her narrow marked parking space beneath the First National Bank Tower, she reflected with undiminished wonder how beautiful and mysterious she found American underground parking lots to be. They fascinated her as much as had Carlsbad Caverns, in their way. She was four levels down, but for some reason the ceiling dripped in places and corners. Dead flat stalactites, she mused. How many thrilling movie scenes had been filmed in underground garages? They contained a suspense, a threat, or a promise.

She exited the car, having to squeeze out through the 18 inch gap afforded her by the carelessly parked Cadillac on her driver's side. Pulling her briefcase behind her, clutching her keys in her teeth and the *Tulsa World* to her breasts with her briefcase arm, she reached back in to the cup holder to get her large cappuccino and Everything bagel.

Suddenly her keys were pulled gently from her teeth. "Let me remote your door-locks for you," came the deep musical British voice behind her. "I can relate. I'm a fellow multi-tasker. Never assign two phases to any process if I can possibly cram it into one, even if it really takes longer. You must be a lawyer!" The dark-suited stranger was a head taller than Cortni. More charming than a Hugh Grant. Able to trump Tom Cruises with a single glance. It's a hunk. It's a stud. It's Dazzle-Man!

"Thanks for the assist," she said, barely keeping her poise, edging clear of the cars, forgetting to take her keys back. "Why is that?"

"The lawyer is simultaneously typing the Jones brief, talking into the phone with the opposing counsel on the Smith case, and nodding at her secretary to tell the next caller to hold two minutes. At any given moment she is handling at least three matters. I think of it as the way anti-lock brakes work: they seem to apply constant pressure but in fact pump and release the brakes in jet-speed alternation."

Oh, God. The man could articulate naturally, yet potently. Cortni had more of Cyrano's Roxane in her than even she knew, because every word was pouring over her like honey. "How do you know this intimate truth about lawyers?" she managed.

"I actually am one. I'd offer to shake but you don't have a spare hand for it. I'm Billy Collins. Solo Practitioner, immigration, international transactions, intellectual property. Fourth Floor West."

"Cortni Justice. Cling, Plummer, and Twicegood. Fifth Through Seventh Floor, East and West and Up and Down. Criminal and Tort. And I think your poetry is fantastic."

"I beg your pardon?" Now she looked at him really for the first time, enjoying his bewilderment and the way his heavy left eyebrow lifted so theatrically. The man would look delicious either under a microscope or through a telescope.

"You ARE the poet laureate of the United States currently, are you not?"

"I do write historical haiku. But–NOT. Whatever can you mean?

"You wrote *Picnic, Lightning*, and *The Apple That Astonished Paris*, and *The Art of Drowning*. I loved the poem about the barking dog–where the guy turns up Beethoven to drown out a dog that won't stop barking, and winds up laughing about the famous barking dog sonata that established Beethoven's reputation."

"I promise you I wish I had done all you say. I do a fair imitation of Tennessee Ernie Ford singing "16 Tons." But now I see I have a famous namesake unknown to me."

"Well, no matter," Cortni said, laughing at the idea of a Brit blessing her little pea-pickin' heart after singing "16 Tons," and beginning to walk alongside Billy toward the garage elevators. "Let's hear one of your haikus."

"Haiku."

"Yeah."

"I mean, the plural is also haiku. Like deer and deer."

"Are you stalling?"

"Very well. But let me hold your coffee at least."

"Cappuccino."

"Yes. May I?"

She let him take it and rearranged her purse and newspaper. Now he had her keys and her coffee. Was there something symbolic about this? Unlocking and stimulating? Hmmm. Billy took a step back and recited:

Dead Lincoln's pension:

Two cold coins over his eyes

Which have borne interest.

"Now," he said, "no nonsense. First: did you like it? And second, is the poet laureate truly named Billy Collins?" Cortni was melting underneath the fabric of her clothes like a Godiva bar on the back dash of a Jag. Must stay solid and cool. Cohere, cohere; solid and cool, solid and cool, she recited to herself as mantras of self-preservation. A walking plagiarism, yes, but so creamy.

"Yes, actually, very much, and yes, he is, and the best one they've had, perhaps. His poems are so startling and witty, but so accessible. He never drones on. And your haiku's interesting because I was just this morning thinking about coins. I was very pensive about it, and then, I thought, I am pensive about two pence. And then that pensive comes from the French *penser* which is 'to think,' and that pence and penny come from the same root, and that the phrase 'a penny for your thoughts' in French might be sort of expressed as 'une pence pour tes pensées,' and then that thoughts and pennies might thus be related since I get my money for thinking. And that's my two cents worth!"

"I am very much out of breath with only my mind running to keep up with your train of thought—a true express train! In addition, you really walk fast on your long legs!"

It was clear he was not in the least out of step or breath, but this was all right. This worked. They reached the elevators, and she realized that in three minutes she had more real interaction with Billy Collins than she had managed to have with her cats in years.

It was clear he had to go. She pulled her derringer from her purse and planted a bullet between those lush eyebrows. A snow field should have no footprints. In her mind she covered his form with snow, and rode the elevator to her office to begin her day.

SIN IS THE MOTHER OF DEATH

Greer stands with Carlanda Carson just by the lowered gate of her station wagon, as she sets out jelly jars for the Future Homemakers of America booth: sand plum, persimmon, crab apple.

"Watch out, Greer, flies and honey, hummingbirds and honeysuckles," teases my best friend Ginger. It hurts; she trivializes him even though she knows how crazy I am for him. I think he looks like Achilles, but that's not it. Carlanda looks like a sleek cow, the lucky kid.

When Greer was four he fell in love with a dead cricket for three days, kept it buried in sugar in a Sucrets tin and pretended a gorgeous fairy would marry him if he would discard his sweetened beloved. He refused, so eventually his mother (controlled by the fairy) threw it away.

Cows would also come lie in his arms, Guernsey Guineveres rubbed with butter to get back out of silo doors they'd slid in to eat their fill. Greer protected their sad, hungry flesh, which craved him so badly.

Greer's a sucker for gluttons.

Tonight he won't escape me for a second. He'll never suspect me of guarding him, since I hardly exist for him.

Carlanda is country, which means she's no Rainbow Girl; she's leaving with a swaying cushioned walk which is water for his eyes and heart; I can feel him flush.

Colters is over in the hackberry trees, tall and yet scrubby borders, with his apprentices Lionel and Dustin, making signs at Greer and Carlanda, all three cocking back and forth like triggers that are just kidding, as opposed to guns that aren't. The faintly darker woods are littered with shredded tobacco from being haunted by sour, scornful outsiders looking for something stronger than fun.

I am too quickly incensed on Greer's behalf. An old farmer with three teeth prods Greer in the butt with his cane and says, "Get busy, boy, it's about time to clear the bulls off the heifers." I'm sure he's heard of Greer but just doesn't know his face.

Colters comes over to Greer, inserts respect in his voice, so credible I wonder if they were only laughing about Carlanda. Can it be they are taking him seriously as a conspirator?

"Hey Greer," Colters whispers, "stick on Carlanda. She'll fuck." He can't *do* it yet, I want to scream. Curse my clairaudience, but double-curse my egregious empathetic intuition. Ablaze with the flattery of the thugs' and Carlanda's attention, Greer pictures new vistas, his brain sharp and jumpy.

Colters will be a welder and make money selling bird dogs. Dustin will be a parole officer after flirting with juvey. Lionel will dance in a chorus line in Dallas, hard as it is to envision given his studied bowleg gait, though he has yet to ever dance a step. It's no voodoo, and no weirder than the graduation prophecies in every annual yearbook.

Greer runs into Meg on the fairground. She goes steady with John Spain but his football coat with the Gold L is not on her shoulders, so Greer makes a stab at her, wretched like a broke doper. No sooner does he offer her his jacket than John appears, the dark mechanic, fuel oil embedded in his biceps. John is casually humorous, teases Greer about pounding him for offering the coat. Greer feels three inches tall, but still walks around with them.

After a while he detaches from them—later anyhow than it's cool to stay. He's hungry for any kind of reflected glow. It never occurs to him in his romantic bulimia that they actually value him in their entourage.

My heart is beating hard because he is finally alone. I know what is in him, the brains and novels that could come, and now so precarious and nervous.

It was years ago that I met him. I adored him for peeing in old lady Hornland's 4th grade class because he was scared to ask her to go; the golden jet ran through the small tear in his jeans-crotch and made a golden pool at her feet. She stepped in it not noticing. I do not know the alien chemistry of this love for him.

Greer loved a girl named Terri so much even Hornland found out when Terri had to ask her to seat him in front of her instead of right behind. After that he still turned around a lot to gaze at her, and he nearly burst with uncomprehending joy one day when Terri gave him a clear candy wrapper with her lipstick imprint on it. Unstrained mercy on her part.

Ginger talks in my ear, hissing intimately: "Greer's alone, don't be shy till you die; he's free and popular." I shake, and shake my head. She drags me right up next to him at the potluck-sack booth and asks him what he got.

"Cannon," he says, holding it up: blue painted pot metal, tiny metal spokes in the wheels. It actually fires lead fishing-line sinkers. Ginger tracks along, chattering; I rate one glance. He doesn't know what a dandelion is, either. Steps on thousands, daily.

Greer is not bad at throwing baseballs, he tumbles four milk bottles with a pitch and wins a creamy colored teddy from the Lions' Club. Ginger's uncle Joe Chain hands it to him; Joe's kind of appealing and sincere in spite of needing braces bad and having them worse. Joe asks him with a voice like a banjo what girl Greer's going to give the teddy to.

"Linda Sarrisota," blushes Greer with an idiotic grin, showing his own braces. I feel like surgery is happening in my chest and guts. With all I *know,* I missed that? There in fact Linda is, walking with Meg. Linda's tall as a state trooper, somehow now with Greer's football cardigan with the single gold stripe on the forearm sleeve. Slavery would be a fair price for this cardigan. Where were Linda's *chains*?

"O God, Mary, there goes your chance!" blurts Ginger.

Who is hanging alongside Greer suddenly but *Lionel*? Ginger is soft as custard on him. Those delinquents can be pretty nice sometimes, and Lionel pulls Greer over next to the rotating barrel ride and tells Greer Lionel suspects I adore him.

Greer's not doing this; he must want a torn ligament for a head. He's offering me a jar of Carlanda's jelly. Third Prize?

* * *

Pins of rain drop intermittently in the woods by the creek on the periphery of the fair.

The fairgrounds are surrounded by a precisely spaced circle of snowball shrubs in bloom, looming like lofty hoops warriors juggling white basketballs; there is a carpet of sheddings from the giant blossoms all between. Most fairs are in the fall, but we have always had ours in the spring.

Except for Ginger's this support from Lionel and Colters is hard to connect up. "Linda doesn't care a thing for him except he's rich," says Lionel. "I think she likes Mickey Mastin."

Colters is actually holding my elbow lightly, and the wax in his black hair smells pink and innocent. "She's queer anyway. She likes to fire pistols down at the police range." His and Lionel's fingers are curled in each other's lightly, it's their thug custom. Such males they *can't* be queers.

Linda's good in lab, wears the white assistant's coat and always has the best experiment, so she is always the one who cuts up worms and frogs in the lab. Her mother's cousin Kyle is one of the deputies; he lets her shoot on the range.

I have never said six words to either Lionel or Colters before tonight, but I know how Greer felt about Carlanda and her jelly. You don't think about the shower of gold getting you pregnant, it's too dazzling and unexpected. I never made a contract to be lonely, most because lonelies set traps and live off bugs and lizards as far as feelings are concerned. So I'll be their Sacco or Vanzetti of the hour.

"Look!" says Lionel. "Greer and Linda with John and Meg, up in the Ferris wheel. Fresh as a banana split!" They are the only ones on the wheel, boys on the outside, girls on the in.

The Ferris operator has just cranked it up and has wandered over to the stale-popcorn stand, getting some. Swiftly Colters the mechanic strides over to the controls, commences to jam them on and off, with sharp brakes, like a pinball whiz. Up at the top their seat lurches and swings crazily.

"Tilt!" he shouts up at them, craning and laughing. I don't exist. Meg and Greer are losing it, screaming. All I can see of John is his hair over the top of Meg's head, black as Colters'.

Lionel is doubled over, shrieking with laughter, and Ginger smiles smugly, like someone has just whipped a guy who'd whistled at her: a dream face on her which I don't recognize.

The operator just stands gawking like everyone else, holding his popcorn so some of it falls to the earth. "Hey Greer!" calls Colters. "Hey, I thought your Mama would have taught you to say Pardon Me and I'm sorry. Say, 'I'm sorry I'm a shit-ass, Mary.'"

"Kick your ass, Colters!" John shouts.

"Tell Greer the Queer to *say* it, before your foot winds up in your motor mouth, Spain!"

Colters jams the machine forward, then in reverse. Meg pitches out over the safety bar. Linda lunges and just catches her by the ankle– Meg's dress hangs over her head like a parachute, revealing her full legs and underwear. Linda has on short sleeves and in contrast to Meg's soft legs the tendons and veins in Linda's arms are ropy cables like Colters' from his welding. Meg is screaming and crying as Linda and John haul her back over the safety bar and into the chair.

I can't stand this. Colters looks white now, strides off from the levers, automatically swaggering though frightened.

"Ginger, I never asked for this."

"He was sticking up for you. If he's your friend, he makes sure you get even. Your old knights you're always loving up in King Arthur did the same thing, didn't they?" But Ginger is scared too, and her words sound like tin bells.

Colters reaches my side, his composure regained. He stops and brushes my hair out of my face with two hands, the pores in their fingers lined black with lube-oil. He quickly slides the ribbon-tie from my ponytail and encircles his swollen bicep with it. "Wish me luck," he leers, sweetly if leering can be. His eyes haven't looked at mine yet. A burning like a dose of niacin flushes down my body.

I feel past *wishing* I was a million miles off; I *am there*, still in a dream. Ginger actually walks over to the underside of the bleachers to see John and Colters fight. Greer's vanished and I notice Linda and Mickey Mastin getting into the rotating barrel together, farmers clapping her on the back. Nerves of a blue ox in her.

There's a slight touch on my shoulder. "Mary," says Greer, shaking, eyeing the shadowy forms of Colters and Spain, "I'm sorry I was a shit-ass." As if it was a verse of scripture his daddy made him recite. Underneath, the terror of too-young-to-die.

This *may* be my last chance. But I see like a hawk: it's *my* choice.

I nod, grim and important. "I'll tell Colters." Greer departs nervously, lucky to be dismissed; I head for the bleachers.

SPACELAND

It was in old days, with our learned men, an interesting and oft-investigated question, "What is the origin of light?" and the solution of it has been repeatedly attempted, with no other result than to crowd our lunatic asylums with the would-be solvers. Hence, after fruitless attempts to suppress such investigations indirectly by making them liable to a heavy tax, the Legislature, in comparatively recent times, absolutely prohibited them.

—Edwin A. Abbott
Flatland: A Romance of Many Dimensions

The narrator of this 1884 novel is a Square who lives in a world of two dimensions, and whose vision of a third ("Spaceland") gets him into grave trouble with the authorities.

1. The Doors of Perception

Well, you know, acid is not complete without flashbacks and you will have to get used to it. In college I was a member of a hip subset of the SDS, which is the Students for a Democratic Society, a great big loose baggy monster in the manner of Moby Dick because it sure contained lots of types and those types often held loose bags of a dry green leafy substance.

This hip subset—a kind of pilot fish escorting the loose baggy whale —called itself the Osceola Society because Osceola never was in any Wild West show and he gave the imperialist honkies some true tastes of habañero hell down in Seminole Country, Florida. In 1858 the chief of the Seminoles, Billy Bowlegs, was rich from white treaty settlement with James Buchanan's government concluded in 1856 after his few hundred Seminoles, over nearly 25 years, had given the U. S. army fits with what would now be termed guerilla swamp warfare. Halpatter-Micco, Bowlegs' Seminole name, received a hundred thousand dollars in cash and "owned" 50 slaves including the master diplomat and financier Ben Bruno, who like many intelligent blacks had fled white masters to become the employees of Indian chieftains, but Osceola his predecessor had never owned a slave nor taken a dollar gift from Van Buren or Tyler. When seizing dollars from the pockets of dead soldiers, he threw them to the wind, calling the dollars "the blood of red men." Osceola outwitted armies and negotiators for years before finally being tricked and imprisoned at Fort Moultrie, where he died of grief for his loss of Florida sovereignty. We Osceolans really were more like Bowlegs, who had conducted one last raid and got to make the final treaty that made him rich, than Osceola—we were just playing at being a radical cell, in other words. Every one of us would become either a doctor or a lawyer later on.

However, at the induction center I was asked if I had ever belonged to a group which advocated the overthrow of the government of the United States. I named the Osceola Society. It bought me an extra free night in the Hudson Hotel, costing the Army an extra Jefferson note: exactly two bucks. You can imagine the amenities. The next morning, October 22, a couple of plainclothes Army bulletheads from the Criminal Investigation Division (CID) interviewed me in a bare room with windows on the second floor of the AFEES.

OFFICER GOLDBUG: So who were your fellow travelers in the Mazola society?

PO' ME: I will tell you reams about myself, but not one name will you extract from me through the torture of having to look at your dumb haircuts. None are in the military service, I'll say that much with relief. And it's Osceola, Kemosabe.

OFFICER PURLOIN: You'll have this coif soon enough, eh?

PO' ME: Depends.

OFFICER PURLOIN: Oh yeah, sport. You talk and we let you swing on the horizontal bars, you don't talk, and we let you live behind the vertical ones. Makes no difference to me, eh? But the coif'll be the same as mine, either-or, eh?

PO' ME: The cell's "a fine and private place, though none I think do there embrace." Seeing you gentlemen makes me realize why they buzz heads in the Army.

ALL THREE TOGETHER: Louse control!

OFFICER GOLDBUG: So you wanted to overthrow the government?

PO' ME: Yes. Also: climb Kilimanjaro, marry Maid Marian, and find the exact value of pi.

OFFICER PURLOIN: So did you ever do anything to bring that to pass? Make a Molotov cocktail? Study the layout of a draft board? Publish a little pink newsletter, eh? Pass out pep pills to eighth graders?

PO' ME: We were non-violent. We didn't publish anything because everyone was too busy. But we wanted to see the system obliterated. If I'd had a button that would do it without hurting anyone, I'd . . . .

They stood up abruptly and simultaneously. Time to throw the baby perch back in the river. I heard later these guys were mean as they were dumb but in the Army who knows what mean means? Or dumb?

OFFICER GOLDBUG: You haven't seen the last of us, chappy.

OFFICER PURLOIN: If we find out you haven't been straight with us, you'll wish you'd never been—

PO' ME: So am I in the Army or not?

OFFICER GOLDBUG: Just no security clearance for you, sport. It wasn't up to me, cuz if it was, you'd be scouring the stockade latrine for the rest of your scummy days, Ivan Denisovich.

PO' ME: Spahceebo! I go pray for detente! I like your Yankee barbers!

Wherever they went from there, whatever critical mission, they are sure to have postured like a couple of melodramatic Orkin men swimming day after day through a sea of moribund insects like me, all waving our intellectual antennae about effetely, helpless and disgusting like the roach in Kafka's *Metamorphosis*. I gave them thrilling little shivers of revulsion and they loved it.

Would they tell their wives about me in bed? Would their account of trapping me in their wits' bottles and probing me, forcing me to yield with the interrogative darning needles they deployed so skillfully and relentlessly, inflame the passions of their fortunate mates? Would young

Officer Purloin use his "eh?" to titillating effect on his Submitrix young wife? I could only imagine the depths of passion my interrogation could be credited with provoking. For I knew there could be no realistic hope for that to occur. *The Doors* took their name from a line in William Blake's poem *The Marriage of Heaven and Hell*, "If the doors of perception were cleansed everything would appear to man as it is, infinite." I relished the role of cleanser, Mr. Clean.

So that afternoon about fifty of us new privates boarded a Trailways bus bound for Leesville, Louisiana, still in our plain-clothes, still our rumpled ratty civilian selves, during which ride I slept and read some of *The Good Soldier Sveyk* by Jaroslav Hasek. I surmised the title would make the *illiterati* figure I was reading it for a role model, even though Sveyk was insolent, passive-aggressive, a true slacker. In fact I got no glee from it. And my bemused superiority in bringing it didn't go deeper than my skin. At a bus stop in Texarkana I threw the book in the trash. It was this distaste for the cliché of alienation which convinced me I was no pacifist. I figured I could kill if I needed to protect myself or my colleagues, and that was that. The moral and the tenet couldn't trump what I sensed in myself. Siegfried Sassoon hated the First World War but felt the same as me, and he was brave as a she-bear. Of course he lived it, and I never in my life aimed a shot or death-blow at a human being.

2. Is There Such a Thing As Basic Acid?

I got into Fort Polk, La., at 12:30 a.m.; reflect that I still had hair down to my shoulders because it had seemed hypocritical of me to cut it off. I wore gold-rimmed glasses, another emblem of flower culture. I had one small suitcase in the belly of the bus, a New Age Bible in hip vernacular being the only book since I'd tossed *Sveyk*.

They marched us from the front gate to a pavilion with a concrete slab. You could see and taste the mechanical sigh of relief of the empty bus as it fumed its way through the maze of streets, fleeing us.

Several tired uniformed privates roughly lined us out under the long pavilion, our suitcases at our feet. No one acted in charge. No standing at attention or anything; just to sort out what we could and couldn't keep and to search for contraband and send us to the barracks. There was a whole load of us, 20 maybe, rumpled and bleary, when Private First Class Laughter (pronounced Lawter) showed up, drunk, in civilian clothes with his white shirt-tails hanging out. Though it was late October the night in Louisiana was warm. This was a nasty boy and he came on like a General and I guess we thought he had that kind of authority. He settled on me and my hair and gold-rims, squatted unsteadily, a bead of spit on his lip, pinned me with his red eyes, and grabbed a big bottle of antacid from the mixed rubble in my suitcase.

LAUGHTER: Hippie, what is this shit? This Ell Ess Dee?

ME: . . . No, sir, that's Maalox.

LAUGHTER: Sergeant, take possession of this Ell Ess Dee. This shitbucket is going to the stockade tonight.

SERGEANT: (*a tall black intellectual looking guy in gold rims and full uniform with three stripes on his sleeve*) Ease off, Laughter.

LAUGHTER: Son, you high? This shit get you off? Answer me if you don't want me drinkin' blood from the stump of yer neck!

SERGEANT: Jesus, Laughter. This ain't Charlie. Save it for Charlie.

LAUGHTER: He loves Charlie, don't you, hippie? They got a porn film out with Hanoi Jane humpin' Ho Chi Minh that all the hippies are watchin' in the Ess Dee Ess while they're hopped up on Ell Ess Dee. Don't they, hippie? You done that, hippie?

SERGEANT: Leave him the fuck alone now, Laughter. He's not exactly scared shitless.

LAUGHTER: This shit ain't allowed, hippie. I'm taking this May Locks, and you better hope it ain't Ell Ess Dee. I'm gonna be in your shit the whole time, boy.

Then he leaned over the edge of the concrete slab and barfed on the grass. When he was done retching he trundled off, still clutching the Maalox. I never saw him again but somebody said a couple of days later that he got busted down to E-2 for hassling me. What got me was that the dumb cracker nailed me even that close on the SDS and the LSD. Where would he have even heard of the SDS? It aggravated my pride, deflated my delusions of being in a cryptic vanguard.

That night we slept in the temporary barracks for the first time. They had eight of us in single-story bunks, and they made a fireguard list. Each of us had to take a one hour shift staying awake so we all wouldn't be asleep and burn up in case of fire. I drew 3-4 a.m. I had on the uniform and combat boots they'd given me after Laughter left, and I was sleeping in them on top of the blanket. When the 2:00-3:00 guy woke me up, I started walking around the perimeter of the linoleum floored barracks, setting my heels down hard with every step to feel my boots. I guess we were all so lowly and whipped that no one protested that I was making a huge noise with my boots, because I did that for a whole hour, never dreaming I was keeping them all awake. Just enjoying rubbing in the robot feel. The next morning they all complained, but no one seemed to know it was me who did it, not even the 2:00-3:00 guy. Could I have possibly been so intimidating that no one wanted to upbraid me to my face about it? Me? Me, neither lover nor fighter? Shake my faith.

The next morning after formation, the intellectual looking sergeant was issuing more equipment while at the same time we stood in line and got inoculated with some kind of new gun that fired the serum through your skin. It left some guys bleeding a bit, a long trickle of blood.

"You hear what happened to that drunk PFC that hassled you?"

"I've been hearing about it. No one's blamed me yet."

"That's not me either."

"So what's his story?"

"He wanted to go to Nam but they sent him to Korea. He hated it. Asians, Asians, everywhere, and never the right to shoot. A turnip vibrates faster than him." Such a shame. Asians rock.

"I have friends who are turnips. Please don't diss them."

I did not know I was leading a charmed life. I ended up in Germany.

3. The White Wolf in the Black Forest

He was SP4 Howard Gunther, but embraced his nickname of Wolfie. We were in a room in the L Troop barracks, smoking hash blended with Kools. Other heads had been telling me this guy from Oklahoma City wanted to meet me, he'd heard of my interest in the occult. Wolfie was about five-seven with pale skin and a large shock of black hair. Everyone else in the room but us two Oklahomans was black-skinned and very tall; at six-two I was the next shortest peak in the range.

Wolfie fixed me with the same glazed, intent look the Scientologist son of Mr. White Jazz had sent me in the college café when he was trying to entice me with Getting Clear With Dianetics. The preternatural arousal of the dead by the scent of Fresh Meat.

"I never really sleep," he announced, his face searching mine. "I know this countryside like the back of my paw." He held up his hand, which was hairless like the rest of him; he had German features but I suspected some Native American influence in his lack of beard or body hair.

"At night I turn into a wolf. All I see of my wolf body is snow white; most of my brothers and sisters are dark gray. I am not their leader but I am nearly as high up in the pack. We have a den in a cave about ten miles from here. One night we were hunting a deer and the chase brought us right up to the hill just south of the base."

"So when you're a wolf do you know about your life as a 'head' in Bad Hersfeld?"

"Oh yeah. I turned on the other wolves."

"You what?" I knew he meant got them stoned, much more shocking than species betrayal.

"Here's how I did it: I go to sleep with a dime bag of hash in my teeth. I stick it to my face with some scotch tape which'll be easy to rip off with my paws. So when I find myself out in the woods under the moon, I've still got the baggie in my jaws!

"So did you also tape your pipe to your snout?"

"Nah. I had pre-crumbled it. So we go out in the forest and there's this German guy and his girl making it in their sleeping bag next to a fire. They've arranged a rock campfire, see? So we attack and scare them off; I'm one of the biggest so I make sure they get away without getting bitten. Well, one of the rocks is flat with a little indentation, so I hold the baggie with my paws and tear it open with my teeth on top of the rock; then I scooch the crumbles of hash into the little hollow in the rock. I grab a stick from the fire; one end is aflame; and I carry it in my teeth and light the hash. When it's going good I blow the flame down and start inhaling the smoke.

"So the lead wolf, Moondog, comes and nuzzles me, and I tell him to inhale the smoke in wolf talk. It's made of barks and pants, is wolf talk.

Then some of the others inhale it and pretty soon we're stoned as shit. "'Deer-ripper,' says Moondog—that's my wolf name because I love to hunt bucks and eat raw deer meat—'what is in this smoke?' The moon in the sky looks like it does in the lake! It shakes and quivers! And I don't smell the man smell around here any more, and my paws are numb and my eyes itch. I look up in the stars and see the rabbit I ate this morning, fresh as a daisy. He says he'd like me to eat him again. This is not expected!

"So some of the other wolves were smaller so they were even more stoned 'cause we did that whole dime and a wolf brain is smaller so it really hit them harder than Moondog. I started growling in rhythm, to the tune of Dylan's "Subterranean Homesick Blues," and they all picked it up and growled with me, 'cause they do what I want. I'm not the lead dog but I'm kind of the *shay-man*. The witch doctor. So Moondog is getting jealous of me, so he says we need to catch a bear so we'll have meat for a long time. So I see that one coming. He's going to set me up for Big Bad John Bear—'A mighty blow from a big right hand. Sent a Oklahoma fellow to the Promised Land. Big John—Big Bad John'—the Bear, you know?"

Wolfie laughed his falsetto laugh.

"So was there really a bear hunt?" I asked.

"Oh yeah. What a bad joke. Everyone was stone crocked. When Moondog saw him he forgot he was supposed to set me up. He attacked and got creamed. So now I'm the head of the pack AND the shay-man. None of the others except me were as stoned cause Moondog hogged the smoke 'cause he was the lead dog and so he did it because he could. I was just as stoned but I'm used to it so I can function like you'd never know."

"So tell me, what happens when you're moving from man form to wolf form or moving back? And do you control when?"

"I control it at night, but I am always back before dawn, that's really true about beating the sun. But at night I can come or go at will. When it happens it's abrupt. I just think it and I'm there. There's no in-between that I know."

"So what happens if you're a wolf in the sunlight?"

Wolfie took on a look of deep drama and doom. "I'd turn back into a man in the pack. Moondog would kill me."

"So how do you know this?"

"Because one night before I found the pack I stayed out still the sun came up. I didn't know that would happen. I was naked as a jaybird, and I had to lie out AWOL all day till I could be a wolf again at night and think myself back into my bed. There was something scarier than that, though."

"What?"

"The dumbass First Pig never missed me, but the guys said I was in my bed in the barracks all day. They thought I was stoned on smack or something. They kept taking my pulse. So how could I have been out in the woods and in my bunk at the same time? That's what scares the shit out of me. I'm never going to want to try to have to solve that puzzle again."

I began to believe he believed what he was saying.

"So have you ever tried to teach anyone how to do this?"

"I don't know how I do it myself."

"When's the first time you did it? What did you do special?"

"I started doing it in Montana, which is where I went to junior high before we moved to Oklahoma. I thought I was dreaming the first time. Like, suddenly I was out in the night in January in Montana, and I didn't feel any cold anywhere except my eyes, and I was really hungry. I remember I kept wondering how I could get to the hamburger meat in our refrigerator. I wanted to put salt on it and eat it raw."

"So what had happened before you went to bed? Anything specially good or bad or strange?"

"I was reading this book called *The Egyptian* by Mika Waltari. And suddenly I had this weird vision that I was being stabbed under water by a foreign soldier, and I was in the Nile River, and I could look up through the clear water and see the soldier stabbing me with a spear, and I had no weapon, and I was drowning and being stabbed to death at the same time, and I was really calm, too calm, and I was an unarmed victim. So when I was having this dream it was like I was watching myself, and the me that was watching was getting really pissed. I mean furious. I was mad at the soldier and mad at myself for just taking it. And then suddenly I was out in the cold forest craving raw burger meat. When I saw my paws, and then when I saw my fur and felt my fangs in my mouth I knew I had gone into the body of a wolf."

You hear about guys who claim that they were outside their bodies watching themselves kill someone. You hear about the psychologists going into to court to tell the jury about how that's called "dissociation." So why not? Wasn't this a universe of affinities? Weren't people a corporation of cells physically? Weren't they a corporation of faceted ego traits mentally and emotionally? Couldn't part of the mind or persona "go back" and separate out, go renegade, go back to nature, go wild, go natural, while the rest of the board of directors stayed conventional, "human," "civilized?"

"So, Deer-Ripper, I think I believe this. But where's it going to get you? You're having these wild nights, but you can't take it home. Wouldn't you really rather drive a Buick?"

"What do you mean?"

"The adventure is amazing at first, but doesn't it get old? I mean, what can you do as a wolf except bite hard and die young? Isn't normal more fun in the end?"

"No. But I also don't have a choice."

"I thought you could go in and out at will."

"I can go out at will. Sometimes I go in whether I want to or not."

"Why?"

"I'm in bed asleep. I just go."

"Let me ask you something. Are you glad you do this? Do you wish it would keep going? Or would you like to see it stop so you could sleep?"

"I just wish I had a girl friend. If I had a girl friend I don't think I'd do this. But you know it's so fucking dull here. How do you keep from going to sleep if this is all you do? I can talk first hand about killing and eating a raw fresh deer. I can't talk to these German girls about it. They don't sprechen Englisch, and if they did they'd just want me because they think I dropped acid when I talk about wolves. Fuck." He shook his head.

"Didn't mean to bum you out."

"I *get* sleep. When I'm gone my body's really sleeping good. It's my head that never sleeps. Probably a lot better than if I just stayed home and dreamed. I'm healthy as a h– . . . as a wolf. Ha ha. I like the brothers in the hunt. But I like the brothers here. I like *you*. You fucking listen. You're not just trippin' off me. But I hate this goddamn place. I can hear the Nazis clankin' down the halls, beatin' up queers with their rifle butts. They kept their guns stacked in those racks in the halls, and they killed a guy if he jerked off and buried him with a pink badge on. I swear I have seen it and it all drives me nuts. I can't shut it out. So maybe that's why I get out into the wolf–so I can shut it out and sleep."

"You're psychic too?"

"I hear the Nazi troops. You can call it that. They are in fact here. They are here. I mean here right now. Nothing is ever over. You just have to be the right radio to pick it up. I can't shut it out at night."

"You do need a girl friend." Wolfie was getting very agitated. His hands clawed at the white skin of his forearms; he pulled out a Kool, crumbled some hash, emptied tobacco and hash onto a paper and rolled it up into a joint. His fingers were deft and competent, really long for a short person. "You ever play piano?" I ask.

"How did you know?"

"Didn't. Just looked at your hands."

"I still do but they don't have one here on base."

"Not at the EM Club?" I had never been. When I made Spec 5 I went to the NCO Club. It was squalid enough for anyone who preferred decadence to action.

Wolfie may have been thrilling on his wild night tripping, but he was not a happy man. It was getting beyond him. His fascinations were eating him up. So, entirely contrary to the dark futurist I imagined myself to be, I felt like helping him. Which in fact happened to me all the time in spite of my darkest intentions, this desire to help. But in helping him, I found out how lame drugs are compared to what I call *journey trips.*

William Blake was the one who turned out to be the inspiration for my strategy, and who turned me from hallucinogens because his visions came naturally: and it was he who burned out of the past to catalyze my experience with Wolfie. Specifically it was Blake's dare-painting *The Ghost of a Flea* on a mahogany hardwood panel using gold, sugar, gum and glue as his tempera ingredients. Nothing else he ever painted or wrote was quite like it. The dare was by his friend John Varley, a painter and astrologer, to paint one of the many apparitions Blake saw every day of his life. Varley asked him to sketch what he saw at that very moment, and Blake obliged, making two sketches because just as he had sketched the first sketch, the creature opened his mouth, requiring a second.

I do not remember where I came across that account in my college career, but Varley's published narrative about the painting's genesis is what grabbed Wolfie when I told him the story and read him Varley's words. Though uneducated, and garrulous, Wolfie could grasp things. He kept surprising me and challenging mere erudition's value.

The flea told Blake as he sketched its soul that "fleas were inhabited by the souls of such men as were by nature bloodthirsty to excess. It was first intended," said the flea, "to make me as big as a bullock; but then when it was considered from my construction, so armed—and so powerful withal, that in proportion to my bulk (mischievous as I now am) that I should have been a too mighty destroyer; it was determined to make me—no bigger than I am."

In this image, the flea's ghost drinks blood from a bowl and has a form more ghastly than any flea or demon. Wolfie found the form of the ghost riveting.

He was the acolyte of one smart college-degreed hash and hallucinogens dealer from the University of Michigan nicknamed Lotus. Wolfie made deliveries in the barracks for Lotus and stoned for free. Although he seemed callow and clueless, there was a fair slice of poetry in his descriptions of the moon, of the clustering of the pack at night—of their music and language. He said his experiences were not a cartoon, that they were human-like in some ways but not others. They would howl if a wolf died, but then there was no mourning and the dead one was absolutely and quickly forgotten. The wolves of his acquaintance were not bloodthirsty or especially ferocious. They hunted smart and ate reasonably, mated and slept and avoided humans. Didn't seem like a wild strategy to me.

I told Wolfie that the hash was superfluous, just clogged the vision. "Look what happened to Moondog," I said. "If you don't evolve, you get gross and corrupted, and you'll go from wolf to flea."

"How come?"

"The more blood you drink, the less you need. You swell like a tick or a flea. You can't even think unless someone gives you some blood. The demon thing is a trick. You imagine you have all these powers, like when you're first rushing on hash, then you soon realize it's less than zero, nothing at all, then you spin down. Wolf to flea to cancer cell to nothing at all. It's a waste. Blake wasn't tripping on what he saw. He was a reporter and he didn't lose himself in the movie."

"Oh," Wolfie said, somewhat downcast. "Yeah."

"So I mean, acid's the thing." S.T. Coleridge, Thomas DeQuincey, Tim Leary, Aldous Huxley. First men on the moon.

He brightened. But he didn't come around me again. Yet maybe the advice took. When I got out a year later, I ran into Howard and his girl friend at a movie in Norman. He advised me he was happy as a clam, and was now 'Garoo. He offered me a joint. I accepted the gift. Rude not to.

THE BATTLE OF THE WASHITA

The landscape of Southern Oklahoma is not typically magical. There are usually no mists, no majestic groves lining the road. Too many fences and squares, and borders never logically following the terrain, which resembled chopped spinach, frozen and bagged in plastic in winter, overcooked in summer. But there are a few places that seem to have been grafted on from other stock by rivers or winds tired of passing Bermuda grass and bois d'arc trees along the barbed-wire. Near Tishomingo there was Devil's Den, or Ten-Acre Rock, a mass of green rock cut by the Washita River, with caves, and a tiny rock-formed whirlpool called the Devil's Bathtub. The strange thing was that the park was privately owned. When the river flowed out the downstream end, it was tracked by willows and cottonwoods and some amazing sycamores and looked more deep-south than it had a right to do. The earth even rose over a rock frame to form a lush green wall over the east side of the river, and at its foot was the old WPA camp called Pettijohn Springs.

When I grew up there, the government had sold it to Walter Bruce Grand, who rented out the bungalows as apartments. It was still like the camp in *The Grapes of Wrath*. Walter Bruce kept rents low, but kept the place clean. Rent was month-to-month only, $50 per family in 1954. If you littered, brought in a salvage hulk, whipped your kids in public, let your kids run loose and cause trouble, threw radios at midnight, trashed the furniture, kept your area a pigpen, kept bad-habit barking dogs, stored appliances on the porch, you were out fast. And no open beer or wine in view, even in a brown bag. He was ruthless, merciless, and pitiless as to these things.

There were eighteen bungalows. Twelve were right near the river, six were in a rough semicircle behind. We lived near the river, the best spot except in spring, when the river was often an uninvited guest. I thought it was great, having porch swings with cushions instead of couches, prison style iron beds bolted to the wall studs, everything on tall legs or nailed to the wall. We even sat on bar stools with backs which Walter Bruce had bought from the Oklahoma City USO right after the war. Oklahoma being a dry state, the stools were in pretty good shape and we knew to keep them that way.

On the other hand, Walter Bruce pruned branches away from the roofs, reshingled as needed, unclogged gutters, painted trees white with pest retardant three feet up their trunks, sprayed for roaches, kept his mousers sleek and inoculated—a fed cat hunts better, he'd discovered, contrary to what you would think—held a daily children's police call, kept his well clean, treated for termites, offered garden patches, and replaced rotten clothes lines. You could smell the chemicals too much: fungicide in the showers, chlorine in the well water, DDT along the baseboards and in the uninsulated attics.

This was still before the era when people started building square brick total electric homes, when they put in central air and cut down the beautiful old "White Trash shade trees," the elms and hackberries, to show they had air con and did not need to shade *their* houses. No trees on house and pasture meant opulence, near-sexual as the opulent fatness of Diamond Jim Brady: you could cool the house, pay to clear the scrub brush, pay for the stinking ugly asphalt made in the devil's pitch blender.

But in 1954 the trees were shelter, air con themselves, worth more than cows.

I sat under them, wonderful subjects looming and swaying over me, with their motions begging to be expressed, but, as I could only draw effectively from memory, I drew a thousand pictures on notebook paper of Devil's Den: Jesse James in the green grainy caves, firing his guns at Indian-painted buffalos on the walls, dodging his own ricochets like a dancing crazy wind-devil, mouth open in screaming gales of laughter, Munch's screamer in chaps. It's what happens in art to early ripeners. I drew the rocks, the small vicious bathtub which would grate your skin like lemon rind on the rocks, and I exaggerated the length of the clefts, issuing forth their runt juniper roots, imaged that they were blacksnakes, eating one another for lack of rats, till the winner became a thick barked root. Bare points for snake-eyes, wisps of ribbon tongues darting at the wind like minimalist pennants at a medieval jousting.

Also I drew pictures of myself behind bars. Jail for me was more a kind of hideout, like a cave. My face could press itself against the bars, in the total frustration of natural riches. I could show how I felt when my mother advised me to pull weeds or take down the laundry. It might be a diptych: the camouflaged patricide (Jesse James *actually* shot Pat Garrett dead in the stomach, in a garden whose cabbages shone like the quarters you place over a dead man's eyes. It was revenge for Billy the Kid.) You know what the cartoonist caption is for every mug shot in the world? "No father." "Father no damn good." If Mr. Tunstall is there, Billy behaves. You can take the bet to your booking agent: if the kid murders, there was a hole in the father the kid can never fill. Juvenile judges bray it, no one listens, would rather blame the mother who must've had kids for the doles. The surface is the deepest depth in true clichés.

The second diptych panel: Jesse in the barred cave, inside the paper weight, permanently about to shoot you and steal your horse. I drew all the time, shot the world. The significance of bars is the nature of the brink, which is of pleasure, not pain. The ugly thought that life is pain, pleasure is an explosion of death. Not just ugly; it's poetry lying.

One day I went down to the river to fish and draw. I got down there and I saw a little raft tied to a stump, and on the raft a quilt, and on the quilt Walter Bruce covering my mother. I was eleven, it was 1954, and the rope I swung through the trees on was the rope of Mom and Dad intertwined. The strands were so wrong here, but even I could see that the strands were also very strong. When two fuck and one doesn't care, the face of that one is a lie. It's a lie set on top of the body like the head of a dumb comedian on the body of David or the Thinker. Not here. Her face was a true story, and so was Walter Bruce's and you could see right there that neither had a hold on the other. It was a wonder and a horror I didn't know what to do with. Dad should shoot him, she should kill herself, they should vanish together in their reflections on the river, I hated, without knowing why, all three, but also I adored them.

Walter Bruce would hold the great police calls for us. Every morning he was like a low trumpet with a medium clear voice, emerging from his separate small house set much further back in the woods, holding a pouch we knew to be full of dimes. We would line up in a long ragged line, exactly 30 of us. "Hungry as a flock of Judases turned reliable," he'd joke in his voice which swung deep enough to be in a soul chorus. He was high and lean, a judge's eye in a peckerwood's face. We would seize little bits of foil gum wrapper, cigarette butts, pieces of glass, tire-biting nails which might merit us an extra dime for saving a puncture. "Fine!" He'd yell. "Picked clean as beef bones by buzzards! Shining like the gold roads of Paradise! Neat as a graveyard!" Its cadence sounded like the opening of Superman on TV—the speeding bullet, the locomotive, the single bound—which we heard weekly on his TV. For once a week he'd invite us to watch it on his, the only TV in Pettijohn. He'd pull it out on his porch, turn it facing out, move the rabbit ears around to get the optimal picture, and we'd sit on the ground before the porch, the Bermuda grass beaten dead blond with our shoes and butts, and watch Jimmy get caught in midair by Superman.

Mom was tall and slender as I am today, brown and muscular, big-breasted, face with strong cheekbones that you could say neither beautiful nor not: which is a gray squall-line moving across a blue sky? She stormed at my father constantly, but in thunder so far away I never heard it. She would make him writhe when she found his character wanting, and he was loyal and silent as a much bigger dog, and he took it and nodded. She grew and sold every kind of vegetable and plant, traded them for flour and cheese, had people coming out from Tish for her produce. She kept rock salt in a shotgun for thieves, which she quietly used to protect her melons. Melons she would take to town and sell from the back of Dad's pickup. Her thumb was green; she never spoke much to me. She would indicate by sign, like the Delphic oracle, who neither explained nor demonstrated, but showed by a semaphore. If she picked up a spade, I picked up a hoe. If she opened a cabinet door which held the trash, I emptied it.

Dad worked in the Pure Oil fields. Although I had my patricidal fantasies as I said, he didn't give me so many orders as Mom. When he did I resented and obeyed just as with Mom, never mind the beer and his chastisements at her hands, that was a world beyond, you just did eat it and obey in time. He told me a thousand tall stories, about how Billy the Kid shot a *mestizo* named Federico Omega Cone in the cabbage patch Mom had, with the cabbages silver and flat as quarters. He said it had been a cabbage patch established by his ancestor Tishomingo, the great Chickasaw chieftain, in 1851, a year before he founded the town Tishomingo. Tishomingo's gift was greater agriculture, as Sequoya's was written language to the Cherokees. He said that nothing but fat silver cabbage quarters had ever grown there. He said that snakes guarded it from groundhogs and cows, so that it never needed a fence, until the day that Billy shot Federico in the eye. Then it lost its medicine, and now needed the chicken wire fence. The snakes had no heads; all through the patch around Federico's corpse in the dead center of the patch were dead blacksnakes and king snakes missing their heads. Billy, he said, was too dumb to be scared, but he had less than a month to live and everyone else, including Tishomingo knew it. They also knew that Federico was a holy *brujo* and not just Tishomingo's hired deputy.

Mom laughed tightly at Dad, and called this a hell of a crop to grow in among cabbages. But she didn't think much of him. Tishomingo was from Mississippi, she said. And Dad drank beer on the rigs, and even though he was good on the rigs, there were accidents. The way I think of it now is wrong medicine, like the cadences of the physicians. Mom needed a strong lance to climb, and a mirror image of herself to climb it with. Dad liked to slither along, his light under a thousand different bushes, and listen to the stories of the rats, the rabbits, the dogs. He was the snake with no ears but clairaudience, and he remembered all he'd heard. His was a wonder directed out, there was no thought of what he was because he felt himself of no account. So the drink. And so her for Walter Bruce.

Now I was eleven, but how could I not, having the eccentric romance of a wild Jesus or Cassandra in me, see all this, feel it all? I had a connection with the windy air, and all the perceptions and emotions blew through me till I felt like a tunnel, solid as Mom against the earth loading down on me, hollow as Dad with his tales whistling through, angry at the chaos and yet loving hard as Walter Bruce, a true hater of messes who was in one now.

You know it, sometimes, but your rope still breaks. I ran home, oblivious to rod and pad in my hands. I wrote a big sign on the sketch pad sheet: DAD: I'LL HELP YOU KILL MOM. Dad was the *brujo's* helper. I would be his, and we'd do them. I'd harden my heart. When in pain, seize on allegiance.

The closer Anne came to bare survival, the more she knew to judge things for how true they were. She was down to cabbages and snared rabbits, a thing still heard of in 1954. Frank, Dad, brought home half a paycheck half the time, because he took careless risks, would get laid off with no pay since roughnecks were contract workers. He was so quiet, a wooden nickel, then the terrified supervisor would see him high in the rig, tightening the threaded pipe as it spun at 33rpm, the torque wrenching the giant crescent wrench from his hands, the wrench flying and striking the side of the saltwater tank 30 yards away, puncturing it like an aluminum can, the salt water seeping out. "Why didn't you shut it down first?" A shrug, a look away not down. "Takes time," he'd say to the incredulous foreman. Maverick initiative from worthless roughnecks, no thanks.

He was a quiet drinker; it made him very silent and deeply amused, until, just like when the foreman's back was turned he monkeyed, his brujo stories would spring out. He always started with a question.

"How did Sitting Bull win at Little Bighorn all by himself?"

I was nine when he told this one. I knew Custer. The Cheyenne camp on the Washita was just eight miles from where I had grown up. Where Custer did a massacre once.

"He had more warriors than Custer."

"That's what Bee Eye A says. It was too embarrassing to admit he did it alone."

"Tell me!"

"Sitting Bull was sitting on the top of a Montana mountain about two months and two hundred miles from Bighorn when he smelled Custer. He had heard of Custer. A man with no fine enemies is an ingrown thing. Sitting Bull said to Crazy Horse, *That yellow man smells like rotten cow birth. He makes up things to do out of nothing and then he scorches the earth bare. The whites needed a good enemy for him, he was fine when there was a good war opponent for him. But he leads a lot of men who have a lot of guns, and Sheridan and Grant gave him tons of money. A strange white bunch, the rich aren't braves and the braves aren't rich. But I don't want a single one of my brothers or sisters to be mown down by him. What should I do?*

"And the two men thought hard, then finally SB said—*Send them all to Canada. I will fix Custer by myself, one way or the other.* Crazy Horse wondered what SB meant, one way or the other.

"*If I lose he only killed a little old man with all his soldiers which he brought. If I win, a little old man killed him and all his soldiers.*

"So Sitting Bull sat down and emptied his head, and someone came —he was calling out whether he knew who it was or not for something to take hold of him and either show the leader he should follow or instruct him how to lead. It was to take its spirit and act through it.

"That's the difference with the whites, they want all the powerful attributes of the horse, the owl, the perch for themselves: they want to be wild sorcerers. We want to be taken over and let the animal do what it decides to so with us.

"So Sitting Bull just called and Crazy Horse just waited and then the bees came. They pulled his spirit out and took him flying. He saw through their big thousand eyes and the ground swam below him as if flight turned the ground into a raging river. Then they took him inside their hive, into the honeycombs. And there were drones in there, and they started to chew on SB if you can imagine, just chewing his bits of spirit up like pollen and dabbing a little bit of it in each cell of the comb and sealing it up.

"Next morning there were hundreds of drawn drone men moving down to the Little Bighorn River, smelling of honey, dusty with pollen, armed with sharp spears as stings and senses sharper. When the battle was over they found hundreds of dead bees around the remains where SB sat wrapped for hours in a hide."

He would do what Mom, Anne, requested, flawlessly, good-naturedly, and it was clear he adored her. Neither wanted to lean or be leaned on. It should have been all right. Plenty would have been amazed that she would turn him down, with all the beaters and drunks trying to turn women into pious husks because they could get no help or support from anyone. But somehow he just was not tight enough for her, and somehow she was too good and true for him. He was made uncomfortable by her. She could call up the truth without any words or criticism, just her presence, her look, could force you to see yourself, even when she had no such intent. Its cost was she had no friends because no one lived up. It was chilling to Dad, where it fired Walter Bruce. This is true chemistry, not motion picture chemistry-set chemistry.

It would have all settled out more easily without me. When Dad came home, he saw my note. I watched him read it, the pale light through the kitchen window curtains glinting weakly off the Jax beer bottle he had already opened. He was tall and wiry, always clean shaven—with his Chickasaw blood, shaving happened weekly and quickly. He grunted, and set the beer down. I came out, feeling suddenly very shy.

"Get your things," he said. "You and I are going on."

"You're not going to kill them?"

"You don't want the Old West, Cline. Cut whiskey is better than straight alcohol, and laws and jails are better than ropes. Best of all is let life do the payback if it will. You can't live on paybacks. Are you coming with me?"

My heart was bursting and tears started coming. The funny thing was that I was hurting for Mom, but I was hurting worse for Walter Bruce, who was also a major part Chickasaw. As if Dad were a fair brave, but Walter Bruce a better one. His stories were cooler. They took you way out where Dad's took you a short way in. Or so I had concluded.

This aching for Walter Bruce was an agony you were able to feel even in bad westerns like *Shane*; there's a clarity in how you feel rifled through suddenly, all the taller older ones going suddenly from casually ignoring you to training their eyes on you constantly, breathing hard to catch up to the runaway effect on you, because you are the Child, the one really to be Hurt possibly. Divorce hurts the children…bull! It hurt the three of them forty times worse than any hurt I felt.

The rifling clarity did not precipitate a pure judgment of death on Anne and Walter Bruce. In fact it lifted their sentence, let them walk. But I could not look at them again. It was almost like I had to be Anne's husband since Dad would not be, that is how it felt, and you can crack "Oedipus" if you want, that was not it. How could I live in their house; this would have to be a bad mistake. No dimes, no reverence in carrying the trash bags or carrying in the folding, without what they'd done and were doing like a nail in the foot to keep me back and out. I assumed that Mom and Walter Bruce would get married now.

Dad was there, no hope, no promises, but no pain in looking at him either, and no shame or loss of dignity. He made that system come to life, better than Jesse shooting Pat. I got my clothes and my pencils and pads and drawings, and we left in his truck. It felt final, but it was not.

In the next months, literally of truck camping and bathing in rivers, of pimento cheese sandwiches on white bread with potato chips and R.C. for breakfast, of stalagmite-slow accumulation of beer bottles, I drew more furiously than ever. But it was not Cole Dalton shooting Belle Star for killing his brother Emmett. It was the river, and the tall cottonwoods, willows, pecans which lined the Washita after it left Devil's Den, and the springs which watered Pettijohn; the leaves overhead, looked at from the ground, swaying and cutting and re-healing the air with its liquid minutes in motion; air, water, and fire swirl in motion when you are still and staring; for the earth to swirl, you must move fast across it, or let your eyeballs in their sweeping binocular mode trace its hills and creek beds—and the earth swirling was what I saw. The leaves and air were remembered, those that cupped Pettijohn like the glass of a paperweight world of police calls.

Let's list the received wisdoms: I subconsciously wanted him to control me, keep the pressure on. Instead the stress dropped. Of course I was deeply disappointed that he would never whip me. It meant he didn't care, didn't it? I worked and sweated as a gopher for the eight roughnecks on Dad's rig, trying to fill the shoes he should have filled, driving myself hard, but then he and they each gave me a dollar a day out of their pay. Before long I was making all the log entries, linking the long pipe to the lift-chain, naming the creeks that ran under the ground, the McLish, the Oil Creek, the Viola—as though underground oil creeks

were ships that sailed the seas of rock strata with names whose origins no
one could remember. I also policed the area around the rig; Texaco
always insisted on beautifying the scene, with flower beds and white
crushed-rock paths lined with aluminum weed guards, and wrought iron
entry gates painted bright green and red. It was garish and neat, and I
loved it. Of course I hated it, didn't I, that the roughnecks seemed so
pleased with me; I wanted them cold and aloof, to show me their iron-
admirable superiority, didn't I really. "Sixteen Tons," whose strawboss
hollered damn your soul at the best producer, or Sir Stephen in *Story of
O*.

I would probably, statistically, be a drop-out in the seventh grade
because Dad was itinerant. No, come fall he put me in Alfalfa Bill Murray
Elementary School and paid a woman named Margaret to keep me
during the week. Fridays he'd come for me, beer faint on his breath, but
there, wordless, but there, and not asking about school, either. A good
used car, always carrying me out to the river.

Even now, an acclaimed artist in the city of cities, I will sometimes
encounter someone who is very good at what he does, such as repairing a
truck. His shop will be immaculate, his equipment rivaling a NASA
installation, and he knows and knows he knows, but this person unlike
so many others does not retreat within his excellence like a fortress
against excellence in love or relation; he wants to be seen, to be a rare
bird or fruit. But there is his sensed tragedy; so hopeful, yet not a lawyer
or other predator, not enough of an asshole or egoist peacock—he hopes
naively that his excellence will draw the attention of an angel. And then I
found out that often, it does. I see him later with the angel, and then I
think, why him, not me. There are few shocks worse than seeing an
admirable object of pity unexpectedly revealed as having an angel for a
partner. I am better, more sophisticated, aren't I? So then I know that
however excellent I may be called, I am not that naïf in grace. But on the
rig, and at the river, I was.

School is the time when the oyster must open its shell, and it was
from school that I was stolen. The day was very hot, in late September,
and the routine for the last three weeks had just begun to numb us.
There was no air conditioning, and the flies were more intellectual

simply in the eager way they landed on the opened pages of textbooks. Mom's method was pretty ingenious. You must realize that in 1954, the Lindbergh kidnapping of years before was still an event viewed with living horror, so rare it was.

The teacher was reading *The Virginian*, by Owen Wister, where Steve was being hanged for rustling, when Anne burst in with bandanna and fake six-gun. She had on a Stetson, the bandanna over her face, and in her other hand a bag of what would turn out to be candy. She strode in, yelled, "Everybody hold it!" and put the cap gun to the teacher's head. "I'm Annie Belle Starr Oakley Masters! Surrender the boy to me, or my persuader will make oatmeal with your brains!"

"Well, Cline!" the teacher tremored melodramatically, "I guess you had better go to your family birthday party! She acts serious!" But she seemed a bit shaken. Anne had grabbed her pretty roughly, and even though she figured it was a game and had the wit to go along with the gag, it was clear that she didn't care for the realism of Anne's aggression.

Whose birthday? But Anne had me looped. I thought she and Dad were back together. I jumped up from the languid desk and ran to her. Her hand on the back of my neck was cool. She holstered the cap gun, complimented the teacher on her bright behaviors in not putting up a fight, passed the candy bag down the first row—"One piece per, now"— and we left. In the car, before I could speak, she was talking.

"I had to have a visit with you, Bud." Anne had called me Bud when I was a day old, Frank told me, because my face wrinkled by silver nitrate eye drops looked like Magoo or an oldster.

"That mule, your father, thinks you can do good like this, with him keeping you and screwing a housekeeper." Margaret?? I could not believe my ears. And *her* to talk of someone else doing that? I raised my eyebrows. I had before me the world's colossus when it came to hypocrites, the irony was running off me like sweat off a blacksmith, and I was also jealous and fascinated as hell.

"She's really old and plain," I said. "But what do you want me for?"

"You belong to me. I have everything, the car, the house, a job, a much better man, a garden, all the books, the records, a TV you can watch every night after your homework, and you can sleep with us anytime you want."

I thought about it. Frank had a hard time affording my paints and paper. I had to draw on grocery sacks we stole from the stores. I've seen chalk and pencil works on brown paper and yes they are interesting but it doesn't take, to stay in an austere media you've been forced to use, to eat millet which was all you could get. It could be gold leaf and caviar, or okra and pig's feet, no matter, after that monotonous duress it won't take.

Too young to ask, to know it would enhance my appeal if I did ask, to ask if I was just the maraschino on that 7-layer cake of garden, books, records, TV, car, home, job, Cline the Cherry?

Oh no, I wasn't just the cherry, no. I did not have to ask. She stopped the car at a roadside picnic bench at a curve, Deadman's curve, went over a rise out of sight, and took off all her clothes, this terrifying me, making me sick, although clearly she was magnificently formed.

"Let's get out," she said. "Paint me now." All those layers, and she wanted immortality too? I was really hurt. "What are you doing? I thought you loved Walter Bruce. I saw you on the raft. I wanted to kill you with a gun. I wanted Dad to kill you with a gun."

"I love you Bud, but I have one life, and I can't let you think without knowing a damn thing that you can get in the way of me getting what I need. I wouldn't have done it if I didn't need it, and that's that. I can't apologize to you. It was dead with your Dad and you may not can feel a such a thing but you can still see and get it somehow, can't you? You know what love is a bit. You look at girls sometimes. I want no more than you get when a girl acts like she likes you. I know the man loved me but he didn't find enough in me to dislike to make it interesting, and I can't help it if I need to be interested."

What was so frightening to me was this opened side of her, who used to be so taciturn and short-spoken. She never bared anything, body or thoughts, when she was with Dad. You could say that she was just reflecting who she was with, that she picked up the colors of her men, but that was not it, whether you suspect so or not.

I'd wanted to kill her and Walter Bruce and didn't want to now, and didn't love Frank less by a drop. So you could say that it was not the *bruja* Gretel, five years later my first lover, who first taught me how to walk the real earth without killing anything. When the truth flows out of you in paint and pencil strokes, you realize that as a liquid it does not necessarily place loyalty as a high virtue, though in a fact truth must be loyal to whoever sees it, just like paint must be wet when you touch it. Water takes many forms, vapor, brook, ice, but we forget or do not think of dried water. Paint that is dried might hold the images for as long as centuries. Water that is dried, what does it hold? Truth holds no images, does not last, because it needs to be liquid in the moment to be truth. You can learn from old history and old art but nothing from old truth that has no water now. Torture one more thing out of this: you want truth's water to hold, you mix it with some earth, and that's paint, ink on the page, what have you.

I did paint her. I tried to paint her doing a thousand things at once: listening to Brenda Lee on the radio, washing laundry in the river like a figure from Bible tales, Hagar or Tamar, being covered on the raft by Walter Bruce, laughing at one of Frank's airy meringue tales in spite of herself, the way she sat like a stone and cut space like a leopard, the way she was so practical with money and her mind always the fastest. Her form and her wit were a statue of Unfairness, hearts eaten out. Her face was thin and hard set with her will. You did not think of angels, though she was purer than many who evoke them. She was not so thin on closer look. She tended to be voluptuous in the teeth of her hardness. But in my painting, next to her realistic image, sat another Anne in the precisely same posture, but thin as Lincoln, all bones and long flat muscles—a twin next to her, not in her, is how I saw it. The park bench, the dirty roadside Bermuda grass, the gravel of the turnout, I made as photographic as I could. I went for the litter of Hostess wrappers and Royal Crown Cola bottles, the ants and the amazed tangle of bois d'arc branches with eastern red cedars. Every one of these things around them and about them was the same, though placed in no symmetry, except the second take on Anne. I made both natural colored. No cheap Picasso thrills.

No, no way she could just be reflecting who she was with.

An eleven year old sat and painted her as would Matisse or Degas, and lost himself in it, and she sat posed like a model—where did she learn it, not catching rabbits—and he did not dwell on the biblical embarrassment of her body or the ill ease or shame that might be found as a spoilant in the pigment of his imagination; he painted her like she was a bee or cloud or road. Who was this kid? The Dalai Lama or someone? But what I thought then was, how could she steal me, drive a few miles, and do this? And what for? Divinity or perversion is what I ask now. Then it was: is she being dirty or just doesn't give a damn? Asked in fear and some thrall, but a thrall that left me freer. This was my best work, the first of my adulthood, though I was just eleven.

I felt like if I stopped painting before she got dressed, I'd be swallowed whole. I felt terrified to speak to her, afraid that she wanted and expected a deeper male voice that I did not want to even have to offer her. Where was Walter Bruce? I was not eager to rise to this occasion. I shuddered that his thin face would melt into something lurid and beckon me; she seemed a stranger, someone ravenous and indifferent whether her prey was me or another within reach. I was as a mouse to her, but I could not feel in her any inhibition against harming mice like me for amusement. There is an old fashion photograph depicting a group of beautiful young women in evening clothes, smiling as one holds a lethal hat pin poised between two exquisite fingers. A tiny miniature man in top hat and tails kneels on a table before them, pleading to be spared, his back to the viewer, his anonymity making him Everyman. Or no man at all, which was me, the world's most callow Odysseus.

We heard the gravel spin over the little berm which hid us from the road. She leaped up and threw on her pants and shirt, wadding her bra and panties into a ball and sitting on them. I blew on my canvas and dropped the tacked cloth over it, began nervously putting away my paints. I went over to the water drinking fountain, made of sandstone and limestone rockwork, and washed out my brushes, letting the pastels drain in till their color faded to clear.

CRIPS AND BLOODS

With a gray-gloved hand Cline pushed a button on the arm of his souped-up wheelchair, and its hydraulic mechanism elevated him to near the top of the blackboard, level with the middle rows of the up-sloping amphitheater. His denim shirt and carpenter's pants were dark blue still but covered with paint drops and splotches. The metal x-braces kept emerging impossibly from their slim axle compartment. Plata's loon-laugh soared high above the rest of the applause and chatter, and she quickly began sketch Cline in the contraption.

He heard the laugh without spotting the exact source, and suddenly felt that his whole show was an attempt to accord his sub-waist numbness a character, a personality, on a good day a cult status, even. This was just fancy pantomime of denial performed to impress a Punch and Judy audience of post-adolescents. Then he laughed aloud, thinking, great time for a miserable epiphany here, next to the ceiling and it's time to dazzle, fly around the room or something. *All eyes on me. So it's showtime, Buck. Throw the knives at the lady.*

And the class, which was pretty much into it, as it happened, laughed with him without knowing why, pretty excited, pretty responsive, and so he did what made people like him, shrugged, got back into it himself with no self consciousness because it was good of them, being ordinary circus-lovers.

The circulars Plata had read, nailed to the inevitable construction site fences, dubbed today's lecture "Gallery Hanging." (Yesterday's had been "Leeching your Canvas.") Plata came in a business suit with her small polished leather portfolio case, her response to the camp cynicism she'd expected to flesh out Cline's performance. In this gray suit she nevertheless sprawled and stretched out unconsciously as ever in her wooden swivel chair, almost lying in it, as if in her pajamas instead.

"No, I am not Latino," she would say. "I am Iceni." And she would explain that Iceni were the dark stone-erector precursors who taught the conquering Celts and later Angles all they knew about stars and tides and animal conversation. The Greeks of Ancient Albion, she'd announce in her melodramatic male-cognoscente-mimicking alto, and then laugh her wild low other laugh, this self-laugh more manic even than the louder loon-laugh at others.

There were two overhead screens side by side above the giant eraserboard. One displayed a transparency sketch of a man with stick figure head, arms, legs and feet, hung from a gallows. It was today's theme. The other displayed a transparency of a canvas within a canvas: the outer canvas represented a late 1950's Warhol man in a felt hat, tie loosened, standing before his easel and canvas with a paintbrush and palette, painting a hand which is squeezing a Warhol can of spinach, and in Cline's cartoon the spinach is squirting out of the top of the can's burst lid, above the canvas frame, Popeye-style.

Cline hovered next to the latter screen, high above the students. Below the screen, quavering on the textured concrete blocks, in the on-a-shoestring-chic manual typescript of a subtitle, was its caption: "Pain by Numbers or Kill in the Blanks."

A cultured British voice-over narration droned under the volume of Cline' voice: "A minimalist tribute to the vast, and yet, to the artist, unknown, associative richness of the audience as perceptors."

Cline quipped: "Popeye is trying to say it means whatever you think it means." Plata was continually astonished to hear he spoke with some sort of atypical southern accent she'd never heard. He tapped the wall either side of the quivering caption. "Choose the best answer with show of hands: A: the presentation on this art reminds you of adrenalin on a warm spring morning; B: the aforesaid presentation reminds you of lukewarm coffee and brimming ashtrays in a prison waiting room. All for A, hoist 'em, Zero; B: hands and wavy fingers thick as sea brushes on the ocean floor. Yes." The "aforesaid" had the irony of a country boy talking flowery. This was so odd to Plata, who had a Venezuelan orientation, limited to East Coast exposure. Cline swiveled is neck and torso back to the left screen:

"Hanging a painting in context as sterile as ether makes it lose consciousness; this is the usual get-up of your Moderne gallery."

Here he made a pantomime show of inhaling the more rarefied "ether" near the auditorium ceiling. Then trumped himself with exaggerated effete ecstasy (EEE). Having harvested his students' medium-sized chuckle, he pressed a button and the contraption he nicknamed Nexus (for Needless Exercise in Uncertain Sanity) slowly folded in on itself again as he came down talking fluently.

"The painting *ought to* pace before you, as in a cage restlessly. You can have wallpaper, portraits, tiger skins, bear rugs, floor lamps around the cage; the art will still prowl among them without their distracting you.

"You should be afraid to get too close to the claws of the art. Other art and décor on the walls about it should guard it ferociously. They are blood brothers, pack members. Hang it over blue silk and splatter blood on it. Hang it in a frame made of gilded wooden human breasts with rose nipples. Play a tape of a firing range. Overhead monitors running videos of red tracer bullets bouncing off fog-hidden embankments. Don't let anyone pass out at YOUR show (my competitors use the ether for that)."

The class-bell rang the instant he touched the floor, accenting his virtuosity in timing.

"Bye!" Cline waved. "Paint like bees, not like mud daubers!"

Plata thought she should ignore this acerbic little coda. There was so much sarcasm that could not be ignored. The day before, after the leeching-lecture's extended, not to mention tortured, analogy between brush/canvas and leech/body, he had announced at this time how seeking safe little role-ledges sapped love. You took a role, usually some variant of hopeless supplication such as mentor or nutty-buddy, the one she'd love if she didn't already love another, the one she ought to love, the best man at the wedding that never is; or more rarely, the *beloved*, the platonic and ideally exquisite fascista—Alcibiades, Mickey Rourke, Adonis, Salvador Dali—to go roughshod over you when you want, be the ghost who redundantly plays keyboard variations on your phantom

failure of worthiness. Playing the masked desperado to play it safe. He
warned them not to make love on their backs, since it smacked of canine
submission, of baring one's throat. The sub-missionary position, he
dubbed it. Another exhortation to stay platonic, in effect—really, you
know, *someone* has to be on their back.

Then she wondered, what claims would *he* make around *her*?
Everyone seemed compelled to make claims around her. Her Vet, Anton
Hammerlocher, told her he was the scion of a long line of Moldavian
princesses, all sorceresses, which is why wild cats love him and let him
bathe them every day. Her druggist helped Elvis die painlessly; no one
knew Elvis had throat cancer and that singing days were numbered, even
though he might have lived.

Even her drawing teacher confided that he was Harris Burdick, the
mysterious artist/writer celebrated by Chris Van Allsburg. He wanted to
show her drawers-full of drawings in a similar vein, and all the stories he,
"Harris," had written to go with the drawings.

What they did wrong, she thought, was imagine a face on love,
other than their own—metaphorically put it on a ludicrous face jug like
the grotesque ones she'd collected in Manhattan from nomadic
Appalachian art pickers. You gave love someone else's name and human
locus, when your only love was in fact an unnamed mean little vole, a
deceptively runted one till you tried to pet it. You thought you
remembered its face from pictures, but in the dark, up close, its face was
perfect, a pure replica, weird as a bee's.

Stolen Birds

This lecture stuff did not sweep Plata off her feet. But Cline's
wrinkled callowness, like St. Bartholomew's in *The Last Judgment,*
carrying his own skin, whose face was Michelangelo's own, promised a
certain canonical charm and safety in them. It was something of a luxury
to imagine herself intrigued. It might set her apart, although in fact she
knew this was superfluous, needlessly conspicuous, since in fact she
herself was weird but was not sure he was really very intriguing. His vast
appetite for High Cool was not the most reliable thermometer of his
nature, and there had to be warmth behind mystery if it were not to be
dumb in the end.

She went home to her loft studio and kneaded his likeness into a pale green androgynous face jug, with delicate ears, classical features, unsmiling lips over straight teeth, closed eyes, and wrote "Kore" into the green clay in very large letters below the strong chin. She adored. it for a long time when it was done, unselfconsciously Pygmalion, wondering if she'd like it if it came to real life for her as him. She brought it to him before class, handed it over.

When he saw its title, he lifted his eyebrows questioningly. "It's an earlier Greek name for Persephone," she said. Cline looked at her and said, "Then I give us six months."

"Very clever."

"No, a reflex," said Cline, tapping his knee sharply with his laser pointer, with of course zero response. So wry and arid, too quick and apt maybe because his senses were numb, wit compensating like a blind man's hearing, maybe, but flippant whereas the hearing was nobly touching; so maddening while meaning to be enticing. Six months. Oh yes, like the sun in the Land of the Midnight Sun. Six months of hell with only your consort's red brilliance to see by, seeing by the light of the flames which burn you, then six cool months of darkness alone, dreaming of ice while he cavorts upstairs with your mother, the Goddess Cornflake. Bulfinch had it backwards: No way would Kore get to go back to earth, leaving him downstairs. So intriguing. It was an older man's world she was seeing in his joke, a world of faux wisdom and mother-in-law hatred, of frisky little Nausicaas going ape over weathered seasoned Odysseuses who smirked in response, then went off in their ships where Down-Low was the mainstay. So which of the three genders was Circe, did you say? Yet she saw herself drawn, just like Nausicaa.

This reverie lasted seconds but long enough for Cline to raise his eyebrows. What Plata *said* was, "you know more than I do. I'll say this, though: Mickey Rourke did in 9 ½ weeks what it took Pluto 6 months to do."

The surprise was in the pain cut through his face. And through her heart a second thereafter. She had not intended a taunt, more a flirty probe, a dare, because somewhere in herself she was denying or not finding it as much fun to think that he could be a sexual cipher. Also she thought it might evoke some claim, a protestation of sexual prowess, perhaps.

He did not say a word, next, then, but suddenly gave her a tight smile, realizing (whether she did or not) she saw him as Rourke, not Pluto. He digested this for a few days. When he saw her next he began to talk as if to someone finally opened his genie-bottle after his thousand years bottled up on the Persian beach.

Would she show him her work? Could he introduce her to John Ashbery at their monthly lunch Thursday? Could she come along now to the bookstore to help him find a good complete set of Proust which Movie Actress (a notorious client's actual screen name) had asked him to find her?

In the next weeks, beyond all this unselfconsciously heady impressing, he was acid-free: decent and conventional, at pains to be fair. His faded jeans came out of the drawer, the ones with no paint on them, and he began to iron them, and wear soft shirts from Banana Republic, and Birks on his white bare feet which rubber sabots had sheathed from winter. These perfect feet were luminous to Plata, seemed to give paralysis the lie, to beg for good Roman nails, only applied to them on a canvas with a brush.

In her studio, foot studies from her memory of his feet quickly dominated her easels, hung from lines by clothespins, skewered to bulletin boards, piled in heaps on the floor like a mass grave of studies. Variations—nails on the toes painted red, nails through them, them bleeding; one foot spotless, the other dirty.

One day he rang her bell, would hear of no help because her stairway was double-banistered and very narrow and he could heave himself up with his incredibly muscled arms. She was to wait till he got there and she was amazed how little time the four flights took him. He was not breathing hard at all. She was incredulous and could not keep herself from checking the hall to make sure Nexus, which she'd heard was his wheelchair's nickname, had not somehow uncoiled itself around stairway corners to deposit him there, seated down on the floor. He scooted in gymnastically on his hands, his lower body not dragging in the slightest.

"Whose feet are you painting?"

"Your feet!"

"My feet?" Cline said. "When have you studied my feet?"

"You're flattered!" she laughed

"Of course I am."

"While you slept. Can you feel temperature with your feet?"

"No, nor weight. They are perfect birds for stealing. If I could touch them, turn them to gold or marble, receive the unfelt kisses of the world's lips that the Michelangelo Moses' toe receives in Rome, perhaps the museums would maintain me, and I might not be in the art gallows trade.

"And, when interviewed about my illustrious and immortal feet, I would say that if one cannot feel sensation, one had an obligation to create sensation, and that is what I have done." Aha! The Big Claim at last! thought Plata. Then, he winked.

He knew that an uttered exercise of wit had to sound like a Homeric declamation a bit, if it was the least elaborate, and that it broke the neck of Dorothy Parker's iron rules of wit, that it be a sharp dagger rather than a broad flail, but that was how his wit came, in paragraphs and not in lines, and he had to accept it as he'd accepted the wit itself as the denial of paralysis. That did not keep him from searching her face, not for approval but for repulsion. Plata's laugh felt true when he bit into it like a doubloon.

Living Stencils

In part it tended to alienate Plata, all this giving and no direct asking. Her partly finding him repugnant nagged at her conscience because she decided he wasn't casting the sly lure. She knew very well that it was a conceit, and idealistic cul-de-sac, really an act of egotism, for her to think of sex with him. Falling into the angel trap they set for you. No mortal could get a rise out of him, but she might: Santa Plata.

He would not expect it, even think about it, unless she thrust it forward like some kind of romantic and ideological dildo she'd strap on to set herself apart, to take on the trappings of a lot more power than she actually felt within herself. It only made it stupider that the poet/art critic Ashbery was a real friend of Cline; that Movie Actress was genuine and disingenuously familiar when Plata went with him to deliver the fifties Random House Proust edition; that later he confided not one nasty insider's cut about either of them. Such potency Cline had, what need for her to resurrect his simple penis from the ashes?

Their instant acceptance of Plata for his sake struck her as genuine trust in him but as a lie as to herself being in their league. They were sincere, she just couldn't pin down if there was a liar, yet, but there was a lie, she felt. Then she saw that she was projecting her feeling of them as different, as a rarefied elite, as a reflection of what they thought of her. They probably really liked her because they liked anyone who was normal, polite, not brash or overawed, and not some kind of mental flasher—a big relief and welcome change. Like Cline was for them in a way. They always referred to his Oklahoma background with some kind of awe, as though he had an abnormally real past. "Extraordinary" people seem really to yearn for the ordinary, because they have finally realized how very ordinary is sophistication.

Cline in curator business transactions was four-square, matter of fact, paying his artists promptly. Some of his Oklahoma City artists called him Square, which he told her was what Oklahomans called an honest man. She took a deep breath and thought, I'm trying to eulogize him. Long distance him. Hold my breath and list his virtues. Tell myself it's all right when in fact the head that rules the heart is just a talking head.

Why wouldn't he deal with the fact that he wasn't all that appealing, all that interesting, all that unexpected? Why was she even hanging around him? He looked younger than he was, chairbound unblemished skin, over-developed biceps and forearms, legs kept in tone thrice weekly by therapists using isometric machines as if he were a cryogenics experiment in deep sleep. She looked younger than she was too. She was a prospectus, a self-created net of images, an ideate savant; she had to be one of those shades in Hades that has to drink blood before she can talk to you.

Nonetheless, she couldn't remember the last day she had missed dropping in on him or seeing him after class. She sought him out in spite of herself. She wanted to know how far down his body *and soul* the paralysis went. There was a dark spot in his center, a black hole of mystery, above which and below which she was certain.

Titian

As they were sitting before the easel, he drinking coffee with his left foot propped bemusedly on a velvet cushion like an ivoried Puck, with a mischievous still life of its own, she painting it realistically on the canvas, she asked him why they gave him a Guggenheim.

"Ostensibly to create a prototype gallery which was itself a work of art, a sort of compound canvas comprised of artifacts. The campaign was aimed at the artistically disenfranchised—everyone without (but some stalking) power or money or haute culture, the list being headed by children, hunters, cretins, young black males, piecework seamsters, hackers, and congressmen with a crusade junket pretext of some sort. I made it. You saw it downtown, my frames of carved breasts, my trompe l'oeil slogans and op-art graffiti which turn into snakes or dancers or sinewy musculature, my mirrors and lights and rice paper walls, my invisible W. C. doors which appeared when you touched them and slid into their pockets pneumatically. My hired jugglers and mimes translating abstract art into concrete expressions."

"Is there a shred of truth in any of this?"

"You can't believe Guggenheim would go for it?"

"Did they come to see it first?"

"At my request they brought school kids. I said in my application that the judges should let them decide or at least consult them. The kids loved my place. It won 5-Boroughs public school poll over the zoo and Coney Island. I even have a noncomputer interactive room I didn't show you. The kids go in and watch tapes of actors playing Pollack and Kandinsky, heaving and spitting and throwing, making the paint really vomit, videos of Allan Kaprow and lesser "happening" artists at work, and a live demonstration by the Japanese woman who dips live butterflies and caterpillars in paint and preserves their motion patterns, trails, living stencils she calls them. And then the kids get to go to work. I've made commissions on a few of their works. One 11-year old girl is enrolled in Cooper Union."

"You really love it. You really do."

"Why should that surprise you? Let's make a list of associations of what I am supposed to be:
—Embittered *Rear Window* Perpetual Witness
—Wry wise bare survivor
—Critic not artist friend not lover Harpo not Zeppo.
—Cut it out.
—Dignity not adventure. Jazz not boogie. Adults not kids. Dogs not cats. Plato not Pluto.
Stop it RIGHT NOW!"

The Buddha's Favorite Marx is Chico

They were to meet in this special corner of Central Park at noon, she in jogging clothes. He would keep up with her, piling on stratum after cabled stratum to his bi's, tri's, delts, and pecs. He wore special thick leather gloves and one pair still lasted only six weeks. She shortened the natural pace of her long legs. They both laughed at how Gothic it must have looked, like hulking Karloff and some organ grinder's demon monkey rolling over the ground. They had done this 22 times now in 26 weeks.

Today for the first time in their six months Plata kept Cline waiting for her. Cline felt it like a lump under his armpit. Plata had been late before, but had never *kept him waiting*.

White violets rose from the mulched mound and spilled over the edge of the curb. Cline smoked a ginseng cigarette on the park bench, kept pushing up with his taut forearms, then crumpling again into a slouch. Finally in his tense restlessness he couldn't help noticing a bed of irises which had not bloomed, behind the nearest bench. New irises, all blooming in purple drooping w's, had been set down next to them in flats on the freshly tilled, friable earth. Cline double-braked his chair, lowered himself to the ground, knelt down, and with the quick system of his painterly finger maneuvers had soon divided the clumps into several clumps each and replanted them a foot apart in the bed. Plata had still not arrived. He scraped up some very old pine straw which had blown under the bench and mulched them.

Plata arrived three hours late, wondering how she'd feel if he were still there, how if not. There was still the cold, neutral or even repulsed little pocket still in her she could not banish with foot, hand, head studies, nor with stroking him or talking to him, satisfying herself with his thick nervous arms, establishing in every mental and physical mode his substance. So she was beginning to resent him *a lot*. He was not at the bench, but in a bed of perennials blooming lavender and pink with a curving irregular border backed by a huge mound of spindly red-twig dogwood, the new growth redder-branched than blood. The Moderne wheelchair was set at a decorative angle just at the rear of the bed.

Cline looked at her face. He could witch out this underground stream all right. Two figures crouched together within Cline's corresponding chill, just behind the door in his face, a cuckold, and a confessor with a tonsure. This Plata did not witch out because he had on the mask of gardener legitimately. The knees of his carefully faded jeans were filthy. The ground around him was covered with Johnson grass, thistles, dandelions, and other weeds—the bed had not been made wide enough. He had a thick short dirty root in his hand which he'd used as a spade. Cline had carefully shaken the dirt from the weeds' roots back into the bed. Their thin angel hair roots were pathetic.

"Sit with me on this bench," she said, pointing.

"No, I'm not done yet."

He had thought in an instant of acting proud, cold mirror of her apparent disrespect; or instead, of acting wounded and parental, or furious and betrayed. These stances felt old and tired. Plata said, "Why didn't you split? In your place I would have."

Finally, treading water, he quoted Siddhartha.

"I can think, I can wait, I can fast."

Plata exploded. "What I can't stand about you is the contrivance! 'I can dodge, I can feint, I can pass.' Everything about you is trying to find safe ground."

"It should be simple, like Chico said: you like-a me, I like-a you, we like-a both the same. What you see is what you get." Not much conviction sounded in there, he knew.

"What you see is not all you get, even you don't believe otherwise. You're a happening which I'm not in, and there's *nothing* outside the frame," she spat at him, "you're the artist, you get to choose and discard. So your big lure is still-life."

"Be familiar, risk contempt, confess?" suggested Cline.

"You bet, confess."

"Don't let anyone deprive you of your season in hell, Capricorn," he said, a thing he's started calling her to her puzzlement. "You have something to think about when you finally come down out of the crags and get to be a unicorn, and put your head in the Virgin's lap."

"*Moi*? In the crags? I solicit you, I pursue you, I map you every chance I get, fill in the blanks every chance I get because you are so ordinary, you don't seem to have any blanks to fill in so I am suspicious! Nobody is so witty AND so nice and needs so little crutches for someone who can't even walk!"

"That's right. All to ferret out why you should *not* love me instead of admitting out loud that you just don't, even though you think you should!" She was shocked, he was as hot as she was, tears busted out of his eyes, and would she throw him over in the dead weeds and hug him? It could have gone either way.

"The gallery walls told the truth like you just did," Plata erupted again. "Big cover-up. Pretending you have me scoped so you can stay algebraic, variable, no value. Telling everything while telling nothing." Slashes of subtly colored paint in angry human postures, raising fists, butting heads, seizing ankles, shooting fingers: "Tai Chi In Flames" was how the neighboring gallery had billed the well-matted hanging of Cline's own canvases. Cline was *hot*, though not in money. His money was in flowers, mongoloid though, inbred progeny of Van Gogh, Monet, O'Keeffe. All the paintings of flowers in Cline's own exhibition asked the same question Satan was asking God about Job: If you twist them, how will they look then?

Cline said, "I brought you my diary. I figured you don't trust me for shit, so as you see this goes back years and this is what I wrote six months ago and it is a reverie about you. Your suspicion is really getting me down. I am beginning to think you hate me."

"Shut up," said Plata. She was reading hungrily like it was a letter from some sailor boy anchored in Majorca. Was it possible her amazing passionate interest was really for him? This diary made her more avid than when executing her foot studies. He did not want to break the spell, the possibility of it, so he watched her eyes wolf down his diary.

Oct. 7: She visits me in the light between the trees—brighter than that between the branches, her hair curling with envy at the things which I possess but do not ever share. I do not mean my wheelchair.

There is of course always supposed to be something which I hold back in reserve, some power which she will try to steal from me, don't they all? If I am to remain appealing I must preserve the impression of being a thing held in reserve, not shared, or the challenge for her will evaporate, the interest will not outlive the principal, so to speak. I will not reap the rewards which, as I am powerless, are no longer deserved but belong to one who is more powerful than me. There must be an impression of mystery, wisdom, good judgment. I do not understand why she worries me like cat and mouse, what she thinks she wants, she's a pistol and I'm not. It feels like what a sow's ear must feel like after having been Cinderella's silk purse for a while. It feels like a crude druid fake used to bilk a Welsh tourist. It feels like I've eaten food fit for wild birds and it's burning a hole in my stomach. It feels like a fucking phantom arm. What do I have to do with any kind of love?

Plata said, "I feel a lot better. This is more like it. You can feel permitted to show me this part of you. I insist, Pistol Pete." And she draped both arms around his slender neck, which, as against her skin it yielded its major board strength, she saw for the first time hardly went with those absurdly thick arms.

During spring break, they spent hours in her studio. Plata had set Cline up to do his work in the sunniest corner, and while he worked as canvas, she worked on his parts like a Da Vinci with a pencil, like a Frankenstein giving up his homunculus for architecture school.

She invited him to survey the studies. He laughed, "Do you think I'm modular? One of those plastic Transformers toys, whose legs and arms and head fold around so they become either man or machines?"

"Yeah. I'm trying to fold you into Nexus."

"I think you distract yourself with surfaces. And distract me, or hope to. Spin doctor."

"Me do that? Look at what pot's black! What does your eye-of-the-beholder art reveal about YOU?" He squinted at her, troubled, appraising her as if what she was doing was the worst wrong turn.

"What would *you* do? My mind and hands have to do triple work. I once ran. I once danced and so forth. I ran cattle down a chute. Now I am what I utter. Or depict. It makes me sick that I'm a Merlin. A stock character. Who is in spite of. Heart only on my sleeve, inside me nothing beats. Nexus is a lie. You are not so restricted."

"You think I have a lot more than you?"

"Nothing beats inside me."

"Come on, there is more inside you than anyone. Tell me I'm not standing near a fire when my clothes are burning off my body. Your tongue has an eloquence that goes beyond your elegant sentences and your paragraph wit as you call it. You want it straighter than that? I can deliver: I don't need anything more. And that's even though I do not know a stick about your past. You are who you were, too. You never say why me—why Plata is for you? You've never said a thing about Oklahoma. You never said how you learned to garden so attentively, handling artists like you were taking care of kids in a day care, or dying people in a hospital, thorough and soliciting like that, and I don't get where you got that. It does not fit with the volcanic paintings." He blinked at her. She was long-lined and linear, like her penchant for sequences: infatuating, exhausting and only *maybe* reachable. Oh hell, the thought trespassed like a drunk on his *stract* lawn, what's a heaven for?

"Answer 1: You are nothing like my mother. 2: You'd have to visit the Washita River in Oklahoma, study Custer, then you might get it. What went down. It's coming up . . . . but quickly. 3: It does fit. Volcanos may have grass slopes."

WOODHAWKS

Introduction: Pre-1961

Vic's dad was named by his grandmother, because the naming was too important to be left to his parents, who were every inch the idle nincompoops they had been groomed to be.

The long-deceased grandmother's portrait now maliciously gathered dust—as if biding time for the indignity of *its* burial—in the basement of the Willkie's low-slung house with many pillars, which stood at the end of Peace Street. She was said to have been so full of vinegar and venom that she still killed all the grass over her grave as soon as it sprouted each spring. This was no longer true, as concrete engraved with name and dates had been installed.

The name Grandmother Smyrna picked for Vic's father was Taft Hughes Willkie, after two of the men who fell valiantly before Woodrow Wilson—the single public person Grandmother Smyrna loathed above all others—so much so that she maintained that she almost wished Kaiser Wilhelm had beaten Wilson.

She could never forgive Woody for failing to oppose the suffrage for her gender. Real power, she knew, decrees in privacy. It does not vote. Suffrage did not come till after he was finally gone, but she laid it at his door.

Her fervent prayers for vengeance certainly worked. Woody got his stroke, and his wife and her colonel got the power that suffrage was impudently designed to supersede.

Little Taft had to grow up with other children calling him Taffy. He was forbidden to fight them, and when once he got himself licked by a boy named Stumpy, he got a spanking from Mr. Links the gardener under grandparental eyes and was forced to go to Stumpy's house to apologize for defending himself. Stumpy felt so sorry for the scrappy kid, who managed to sneak in a defiant ugly face at Stumpy, that he befriended Taft, and it was in fact Stumpy who took to calling him Tad.

When he grew up, Taft legally renamed himself Tad, and he also grew up a vocal intellectual Red, a card carrying member of the Communist Party. He funded Stumpy—now called by his real name, Frank Timms—through the Forestry Department at A&M in Stillwater. Frank went to work as a woodsman and organized unions against Weyerhauser down in Choctaw and McCurtain Counties.

When he was five, Tad's fifth cousin Wendell, who didn't know of the Oklahoma branch of Willkies at Kilnville, had been thrashed at the polls by FDR. Tad had been thrashed at the back door, for remaining obscenely cheerful on this day despite a full and fair briefing on the gravity of his distant cousin's defeat—paddled by Mr. Links, of course under grandparental eyes. Those eyes closed forever in 1943, having burned holes in FDR's psychic heart and in her chest was buried a heart that almost, but for the valiant Brits under the Tory Churchill, had wished for Hitler to beat FDR.

When speaking to his only son of his own ephemeral parents, Grant and Enid, Tad usually referred to them as The Poop deck. It's meant ironically, he said. Grant and Enid never gave orders. They never "pooped."

Losing to the Devil was a Willkie family tradition. Tad only made the political Devil right-handed instead of left. McKinley Grant Willkie died in 1954 when Senator Joe McCarthy was fumigating the Ship of State for Red termites. Tad was Grant's oldest surviving relative by virtue of a tendency to early kidney failure among Kilnville Willkies, so he got control of the seventeen brick plants before he could legally vote or drink.

Tad passed up a sure bid from Harvard—he was genius in school, in anything in fact—and went to Oklahoma A&M with Frank Timms. He majored in History and Government. When he came home on vacations he went out to the Kilnville plant to make bricks.

By age 20 he had brought in the CIO for his frightened workers, who were scared of being tagged as Reds, only to find that it merged with the more conservative AFL that very year and lost a lot of its leftist oomph. The workers figured that Tad's generosity alone made them Reds. Reds always pick other Reds to unload their undeserved surplusage on, they figured. He raised their wages, gave them a share of profits equal to his own, and put three ordinary workers—nor foremen— on the board of directors with himself and his new wife Lakota, a full-blooded Sioux from northern Iowa who was trying to organize a socialist movement among Oklahoma's Indians.

She called her cell of post-adolescent Creek and Seminole kids The Uncivilized Tribe; she had gone to the U. Of Chicago—then one of McCarthy's "hotbeds"—on scholarship. Of course her cell-disciples had more red-hots than red ideas. (No, no, no. Red-hots are only little spiced candies which used to be popular.)

In 1953 Tad and Lakota had their only living baby, Eugene Victor Debs Willkie, named sardonically after a third man who lost to Wilson— the classic socialist who once got 6% of the presidential vote while campaigning from a jail cell. When he was a baby, they called him Debs. That's what they intended to call him forever. He had a little twin sister named Emma Sinclair, after Emma Goldman and Upton-and-Lewis, but she died in her incubator.

Early on in grade school he had to live with other children calling him Debbie. He took it for all of two years, at which point he asked Tad and Lakota if he had a middle name. They told him he had two first ones. He declared, "I'm Gene Victor," naturally dropping the "Eu." Tad and Lakota, white and red, thought it was hilarious, the perfect retort to the very idea of miscegenation. It stuck till junior high, when he tired of it and boiled it down to Vic.

Unlike Tad, who was tutored and then boarded at patrician eastern schools, he attended Kilnville public schools. By the way, in pronouncing that town's name, the "n" is silent.

* * *

1961

"Mama, why is Dad lying around in bed so much?"

"Tired of playing back-assward freezetag politics," answered Lakota Willkie. She was straight as one of the cedar boards in their walk-in closet. Tad Willkie had succumbed to comfort, remodeled the Willkie homestead on Peace Street. In fact the house had one of the new intercom systems, wood paneled rooms, an electric can opener, a Hammond organ and central air.

"What does that mean?"

"Say Tad writes an exposé of how the policy guidelines for federal stink bomb purchases tend to favor the Skunkmen's Association over the cheaper yet deadlier products of the Independent Cooperative of Dead Fish Farmers. Well, Tad's tagged them, right? He's got the evidence and the numbers. But it's Tad who freezes, waiting for action. Then the Executive Director of the Skunkmen writes a letter to the newspapers blasting Tad. And he freezes, holding his same cheater's ground. Tad responds. And freezes. One day the freshman Congressman who's chairman of the Fragrant Warfare Subcommittee of the Special Projects Subcommittee of the Armed Services Committee subpoenas Tad and the Skunk manager to testify. Net result: some frozen pieces of prose, a host of frozen-out dead fish farmers, and a mass of unwanted dead fish sitting in surplus government storage. And the people getting ripped off, the workers, could care less. And he's decided they're right."

"Bad news."

"He thinks they want to be slaves. He thinks they should be. He says his brickyard workers are like grouchy drunks who will fight hard in their sleep rather than wake up."

"Is all that right?"

"Oh, I don't think it's that simple to be superior."

Vic put up his ball glove and his blue three ring notebook, in which he had been drawing up box scores and writing play-by-play narration of make-believe ball games, in which every player was a real major-leaguer, but still an amateur teenager.

The heroes were future members of the Pittsburgh Pirates. Bill Mazeroski and Bill Virdon fought over the same 13 year old girl, blond hair flowing over her shoulders, who was the other team's star pitcher, first to break the gender line thanks to visionary owner Ranch Brickey. (She was this girl in Vic's class, Gazania Upton).

Dick Groat was also a detective on the side, who discovered that Team Sponsor Pete Peyola was smuggling pirated rock and roll records into Rio de Janeiro. Smokey Burgess got suspended for kicking a racist café owner who refused to serve Roberto Clemente. Vic grafted and reworked this last bit from the movie *Giant*, where Rock Hudson gets knocked ungracefully, disgracefully flat by a grisly cook who refuses to serve Rock's Hispanic friends. *Giant* was his favorite movie. He'd seen it three times, all 3½ hours of it.

Somehow all this got worked into the play-by-play, as narrated by a socialist announcer named Red Grit, who was often the target of assassination attempts, usually with a baseball bat in dark stadium corridors.

Later, Lakota came across this sheaf of sporting genius in his notebook while checking his Honors-English essay for punctuation—he was a champion speller and the only eighth grader in high school honors English, but he hated commas.

She laughed out loud. "Blood, color, and upbringing will show," she thought. "You're half red in all three."

Lakota still organized, but not for the communists, who in 1966 had less zip than a lizard on an iceberg. She managed a public radio station and also traveled to the heavily Native American Capitol Hill section of South Oklahoma City as a special Peace Corps advisor to the Indian Nation—hoping to help rehydrate the desiccated historical and legal fact that the Indians were nations—even off reservations, which in Oklahoma had been entirely abolished.

LaDonna Harris, Native American activist wife of the future populist senator Fred Harris (then a State Senator from Comanche County) recommended Lakota for her job.

Lakota was not home much. Tad let Vic go where he pleased; Tad had lost much interest in anything beyond the brick fences of their home, including the brickyards, which had shrunk in number from seventeen thriving yards to seven struggling ones. His passions had contracted severely to home decorating, dogs, and books.

One evening in July Vic picked up his glove and bat, and moved to the door. "Got a game, Tad," he said. Tad had never cared for the role names like Dad, though Lakota preferred Mom, having had a fine one herself.

Whenever Vic wanted to go somewhere at night, he picked up his glove. It was like a hall-pass at school; Tad never challenged him when he had his glove; it was his symbol of innocent destination.

"Happy organ grinding, Monkey," Tad said. This reflected Tad's view of any entertainer, athletic, thespian, or otherwise. He didn't worry about Vic's absorption in baseball because he assumed Vic wasn't good at the game, but he hadn't hidden what he thought about it.

"Pro ballplayers are slaves, bought and sold. They grow old and beer-tubby in bars, with less grace than used up soldiers. At least some gladiators were killed when they slowed down." That was Tad's speech on baseball, a decade before Curt Flood's Thirteenth Amendment challenge.

"Huh," Vic had replied with ruthlessness and perfect justice, "what does Tad do? When he talks to anyone, it's about old labor battles, sticking out tongues at corrupt bosses and tweaking red-baiters' noses. Who kills used up Reds?"

Tad loved it. "That's the moxie, kid! No guff from the bosses!"

Vic stuffed his glove and bat under the new blue Arizona Cypress hedge Tad had ordered, which was already burning up ingloriously both through ignorant neglect of its watering and through its being totally unsuited to Oklahoma summers. Then he crawled under after them and picked up his bat and leaving his glove–taking the shortcut and emerging halfway down on their long drive.

"Vic!" Two musical voices in unison. He pounded his bat on the ground twice, hard, driving the demon voice off. He turned from his deteriorating script-reverie to see the Upton twins, Begonia and Gazania, gorgeous in fuchsia pedal pushers and chartreuse pleated blouses with flared Mexican sleeves. Blue Saguaro cactus embroidered on the sleeves. They caught up with him and enveloped him with cologne and exuberance right in the middle of Catalpa street.

Giant-leaved catalpas actually bloomed as far down as could be seen on both sides of the street. Impatiens, four o'clocks, tea roses opened up for business with a fleet of hummingbird moths along Tad's stone wall. Vic knew from Tad that they were moths, not hummingbirds, that had come to the same evolutionary conclusion as hummingbirds, but from the insect kingdom.

"What are you up to, Vic?"

"Going to the fire station."

"You?" cried Gazania. She was as loud in voice as in clothes. Begonia and Gazania were all of 70 inches tall, giving them 6 inches on Vic, who was actually 5 months older. "Who you going to clobber with your ball bat, Red-coat?"

He was currently cast as the redcoat who lost his red coat in the home room play called, "The Red Coat." Gazania was the lead, Betsy Ross. He grinned. He couldn't fathom this attention. Begonia exclaimed that the play was totally dumb. It really was a totally airheaded meringue concoction, as she said, about the cat who ruined the yarn Betsy Ross was using to sew the flag but redeemed herself by snatching a redcoats red coat and clawing its sleeves to ribbons till Betsy Ross got the idea of unraveling it. Begonia was the cat, which explained why her vehemence ran a little stronger than Gazania's.

They seemed happy to carry the whole load of the acquaintance and the conversation, like a fat man on a teeter totter.

Maybe girls were hummingbirds and boys were hummingbird moths.

They were a different world than the boys. They wanted to know about things like how his father's mean, silky dogs, sleek wolfhounds and retrievers and Great Danes, felt to pet! Tad kept an assortment of pedigree watch dogs and never tired of grooming them or of reading Jack London, who was another dog-loving socialist like Tad.

Or they talked about the new Baptist minister, Rev. Canning from Illinois, who drove a souped up '55 Chevy and chain smoked Luckies, and his crazy kid Coffee who insisted he was a Nigra.

Or was it true that Tad once got Elvis Presley to endorse a meatpackers' strike by sending him a specially-made can of meat labeled with a photo of a wretched meatpacker hefting a huge steer carcass, his apron covered in blood, with Ludlow's Raw Human Spam as the brand name?

The kind of questions Mr. Sparington, the new liberal honors English Teacher, loved to get, the kind Vic loved to ask – these girls asked. Real males didn't ask teachers questions. Not a suckup among them. They gave the teachers the obligatory bird when they weren't looking. Except the coach, the shop teacher, and maybe the FFA teacher, who was also the County Agent.

Begonia and Gazania and Vic thought that pretty much the same things were moron. Boys never played with girls at recess; how moron. Vic soon realized that what girls did and what boys thought they did were miles apart. Girls never played sports, except for Begonia and Gazania, which was moron. Girls were good at school and better at Figuring Out. Seeing Through. They just bragged less and didn't fight often. Like Lakota.

Begonia and Gazania were crazy. They loved to tease Vic.

"You're gorgeous, Gene Victor!"

"Yeah, you look like a Debs-u-tante!"

Even when they would briefly stroke his straight black hair, it never occurred to him that they could mean it.

"Where are you REALLY going, Vic?"

"Firehouse."

"REALLY firehouse?"

"Gee, you're red but you're not burning!"

"Slow down! Where's the fire!?!"

Vic looked down. It was funny, but it couldn't be funny.

"There's a big fight down there tonight." He burned with shame, fearing they'd ask him if he was the Brave who was fighting. He felt as if a big red C for Coward burned always in his forehead. If they found out they'd mock him with no mercy, he feared. Desolation Row.

"WHO'S FIGHTING?" yelled Gazania. Begonia, a hair more sensible, shook her rich brown hair off her forehead like Veronica Lake, and ignored her sister.

"Come to the movies instead," she invited. "It's *Goldfinger*."

Vic's mouth fell open. "You get to see *Goldfinger*?" Kids weren't allowed into it. Every kid above the 4th grade was dying to see it.

"We got a deal with Succor Custus. Get you in too."

"Succor knows my folks," he said, wincing. "He'd never let me in."

Vic felt like a butterfly pinned to cheesecloth. He couldn't speak for shame.

"Don't worry, either one of us alone can knock that asshole Scalder's butt in the dirt."

It cut him dead that they knew Scalder Turnbull wanted to whip him. But what he wondered absurdly was:

Could they really do that? How could they possibly. But what was more amazing was that they had not a wisp of contempt for Vic. They meant it, they'd try to kick Scalder's butt. That crazy.

Welcome as their attitude was, it was the mockery of boys that Vic feared worst – after Scalder's own scorn, of course. This was the Earth Vic lived on. These twins and their girl-friends might as well have been from Venus.

He rubbed his bat tensely, pounded it in the dirt. "I might learn something down there," he said.

His voice seemed far away to him. Was he, great-grandson of Sioux guerillas, really revealing this to these crazy girls? As if they were guidance counselors, or ultracool headshrinkers who didn't mind saying words like asshole to him.

"Get behind Scalder and brain him with your bat," said Gazania. "Amnesia would have to do him a lot of good."

"I don't see how you learn just by watching," said Begonia. "Or why Scalder's worth it. Come on with us. Do you think it's true that Succor Curtis is really a woman? I think he's Ma Kettle."

They both hooted. "Simply superb, dear!" shrieked Gazania. "Yes, superb!" agreed Begonia. Their shrieks were brassy and windy, like good jazz music.

Gazania had a fast ball that could strike out half the lineup of the eighth grade all-stars. She'd done it on the sandlot field in front of the Old Folk's Home after school one day. No one was going to ever punch a girl's lights out, or degrade her for being yellow. Vic wished to God he was Gazania.

Like when he was 3 or 4, finding his friends' mothers so beautiful that he daydreamed he was those women. But now it was envy as well as admiration.

"No, I need to get this over with," he said.

"How can you pick that badass over Goldfinger? And US?" they cried, loping off.

Vic realized that he was still staring at them in the middle of the street, like a steer. He walked the other way down Catalpa, and in a minute the old firehouse came into sight.

The Firehouse was a narrow two-story made of brick, a block off the square. He'd been upstairs once, to visit his friend, old Flanders France; with the dirty cots with no sheets, and the open cans of Campbell's chicken noodle and pork and beans lying among the copies of Grit and Field and Stream, it looked some more like a camp of hobo trolls under some bridge than a fireman's dorm.

Flanders was a WWII veteran, with his right ring finger missing. He owned a salvage and dump yard in Kilnville. Vic had first thought that firemen lived full time in the firehouse, but now he knew Flanders lived in a two room house next to the salvage yard, which his wife kept as clean as the yard was filthy. It was white with red trim, and the elm tree trunks were painted white up to five feet from the ground to ward off bores.

Flanders also raised fighting cocks in rows of individual coops, after the pattern of beehive rows, which was another use the engine wells were put to occasionally. His real name was Vance, but that sounded foolish—Vance France—so when he returned to Kilnville they started calling him after where he was wounded and sent home from.

Mrs. Genevieve France used to babysit Vic in her home now and then. Flanders would tell him stories of other famous figures deformed by war and duel—how a Spaniard named Coneystayro shot Billy the Kid in the eye, right out there where that lettuce patch is.

Seeing the firehouse with the milling spectators settled Vic. They had rules that any fight had to be scheduled a week ahead—just to make sure that boys fought cool-tempered rather than hot. You had to shake hands. You could choose gloves or no gloves, unless one boy weighed over 15 pounds more than his opponent. Then you had to wear gloves.

It was safer than the streets.

(They had a scale inside that cost a penny and told your fortune. Vic plugged in a copper. "A business associate makes you a tempting proposition, but don't let him think you're over eager. Take a wait-and-see attitude . . . .")

The firemen figured it was better for boys to settle it in the firehouse than by Chicken in cars out on the main drag.

Or by fighting in the weedy old courtyard behind the Majestic Theater, with no controls.

Where a kid might get stuck with a pigsticker or get his permanent ivories crushed in by brass knucks.

The firehouse was no Police Athletic League gym, though. The firefighters drank homebrew and Thunderbird in brown paper bags and bet their paychecks on scrappers big and small.

Tonight it was crowded. There was a catwalk up over the floor of the garage which connected the dormitory to the dining room, and the firemen in their inevitable suspenders were perched on the walk. The cement floor was a spotted umber in hue from years of tobacco spit.

What was different was the north wall, which was lined with black teenagers of both sexes. Vic had been there three times; never had he seen a black there.

"Hey Vic."

"Hey Catman." Catman was Weston Pegger, who owned a gas station and had twice been on American Bandstand. His hair was still streaming back in the slick invisible wind, his collar still up, his feet still loafered though now the loafers were dilapidated (from sloshing in beer?) And the white socks were gone.

Catman had been the best dancer, the best roller skater, and had the fastest Chevrolet. He'd talk jazz, but he'd never ever fought anyone. He liked everyone the same. But everyone was all gone. He sat in his station, sold cold beer to motorists, and said he never missed his dancing days. He said he was in hog heaven.

"Welcome to the Darktown Strutters' Ball," said Catman.

"Why are they here?"

"Firehouse rule. If a colored fellow fights, they can come."

'Well, who's fighting?"

"Scalder Turnbull and this other white boy."

"?"

Catman laughed. "Last Thursday night Scalder shoved this little colored kid from Dunbar School off the sidewalk in front of the drug store. Scalder said the kid ought not to be on a sidewalk when white men were on it. This other kid was parking his bike in the bike racks down on the street and he up and told Scalder to apologize to his brother. His brother! Him pale as Pillsbury!"

Catman could hardly talk from laughing.

"Well, Scalder was bowled over, and he said he didn't see any other niggers but the one he'd shoved. And this other boy says, There you go again you rude asshole, calling my brother a nigger! And Scalder said, He's not your brother! And the boy said he certainly was and hadn't Scalder, who he called a Diphead Cracker, ever heard of a pale negro. And then he said he'd kick anyone's ass who said he was a filthy white man.

"Well, the little colored kid was half scared to death himself, being only seven or eight. But this other kid was not so tiny, so Scalder called him to the Firehouse instead of whooping his ass right there. I guess he figured he'd better check on this guy who was so crazy. Like to see if he'd took lessons from Oddjob, first."

Oddjob being Goldfinger's sidekick, who had kids throwing hats at improvised statues all over Kilnville.

"What's the kid's name?" Vic asked

"Canning." He of the twins' mention. "He's the Baptist preacher's kid, and he sure could use a good revival. I think he's got one foot in the grave. Calls himself Coffee. Well, I got to get a seat for this." And Catman climbed up to his special always-saved Galahad spot on the catwalk. He was an alternate fireman, a janitor for the National Guard (PX privileges). Catman always had a sweet deal, an in.

Vic pushed through. He had a way of melting in, of not being noticed. Using it, he got clear to the front row of the ring, which was bounded by hemp ropes moored to concrete-shoed metal posts padded with old pillows roped around them. But the floor was bare concrete.

Scalder and Canning were in corners. The light was fluorescent in the firehouse–fluorescent was the rural-burg rage, having made it to Kilnville about a decade later than Oklahoma City. So in this light Scalder's bare chest looked a hair paler and more vulnerable above his belt–Scalder's being a broad worked leather one with "WILD HAIR" burnt into the back and a big silver buckle with a longhorn skull raised in brass.

But his huge arms were ridiculous, 9 inches thick—about as thick as his tough but bowed spindly thighs.

Scalder caught Vic's eye. He smiled as if he loved Vic, crossed his arms over his heart, and mouthed, "You and Me. Forever." And he coupled his hands in sinister union. "You next, dear," he stage-whispered, blowing a kiss.

"That boy looks like a sailor," said a man in a suit near Vic, a man Vic had never seen around. "He should join the navy and sail to Morocco." It was exactly right. Scalder was bowlegged as he could be—from motorcycles, not horses, which he never rode. His walk rolled like a sailor's, and he had a sailor's bad mouth—at least, the bad mouth a sailor's is rumored to be.

They were wearing gloves. Considering Canning, it was easy to see why. Scalder had six to eight inches on him in every direction except height—reach, chest width, etc. And twice the fifteen pounds weight difference which mandated gloves.

"That other fellow should be allowed a glove to wear on his face," remarked the man in the suit again. Vic looked closely at Scalder's lunatic challenger.

Could be Lord Byron, he thought. Canning stood very erect in his corner, not dancing, not feinting or feigning punches, his mouth as level and neutral as the face in the Moon. He doesn't dance, Vic thought, he doesn't jive, but I'd swear he has the expression of a black man. Then he winced at the racism weeding up in the thought. Live among dumb ducks, you start to quack.

He wasn't supposed to believe there could be such a thing as the expression of a black man. But he'd seen it, and he could recognize it, and it swam into him like a spermatozoon unwelcome. It was the look of Cassius Clay or Malcolm X: I am young, fearless and serious. Huey Newton on a poster. The look meant "Here." It meant, "Present and Self-Accounted-For." The look white drill sergeants thought the Army owned when the best trooper wore it on his black face, but which the Army couldn't really even rent. Canning's arms looked like bamboo stalks, hard but thin and glossy; when his biceps flexed in the course of some simple task, they formed a slight hump. Something, more electric than muscular, seemed to support his tall uprightness. He was five-nine, weighing 120.

He was certainly not albino as rumored. His hair was black, short, curly and very fine, and his eyes were pond-green.

He had a small bright blue tattoo on his hairless chest, just over his heart. It was a ribbon inscribed MOTHERLESS. No heart.

"Now that one already *is* a sailor." This time Vic got a direct look of address from the man in the suit. "Sails from Stringtown Harbor. On a ship with neither mast nor master." Vic was startled. That explained the tattoo. Stringtown was the state reform school. "Kid's a woodhawk," the man added. Vic had just seen the same B-Western at the Ritz and knew its meaning. The hero was called that by whites in their covered wagons when he tried to help the Indians fend them off. A woodhawk turned against its own kind.

It was as if the stranger were projecting his thoughts to Vic alone, as if he alone noticed what or who was usually ignored while ignoring the conspicuous. As if anyone but Vic would be too much of an audience, would dilute the intensity of the perceptions he was sharing.

"How come you know that, or him, mister?" asked Vic. But the man seemed to be listening to something else. The black cheering section was loud, jubilant, sarcastic. They had nicknamed him Percy.

"Have faith, Percy!"

"Hit him with your Sledge!"

Vic figured their carnival boisterousness and gentle ridicule hid some friendliness for how Canning had stood up for the little black boy, but they couldn't believe it was real, and they thought Canning was a plain fool. They weren't about to seriously root for this bizarre kid.

The stranger made a move over, like he was going to stand next to Vic and confide more of his disquieting insights. Vic saw Flanders France, and, which was weird, Mrs. France, across the ring. Without waving at them he filtered away from the stranger and moved around the ring toward them.

"Wife's here to do any mending," said Flanders, leaning over to a nearby spittoon to let out some Mail Pouch juice. He was always being clean, throwing away pork and beans cans and polishing engines. His

Dalmatian, Spot, was at his feet as always; the firemen called hound and master Spot and Spotless.

Genevieve France was a practical nurse. No one had ever been badly injured at the firehouse fights, and there had never been any remotely medical person there. She had a look on her face that Vic didn't like and couldn't remember from the kind days he recalled when she babysat him.

The look seemed to say, "If it thinks it's a nigger, whup up on it like one." It was a look Vic saw around on a lot of faces, now that he saw it on hers; it was not far from the look you saw on faces at a high school football game, or at a local election watch. It was not *all* hate; it was partly a fervent identification with What's Us. Us was favored heavily. Us was really looking forward to this. This is Us' life. Apart from this sort of scene Us don't feel like much.

"This boy's from Illinois," said Flanders, pronouncing the *s* in Illinois. He didn't need to say anything more. The boy was a northerner and he was failing to understand the understood. Flanders figured the whole weird world of northerners was from Illinois.

Flanders went into the ring. It was his turn to referee, it seemed. Vic knew one thing: whatever he thought, whatever his wife thought, he'd be fair and he wouldn't let Scalder slaughter Coffee.

There was no bell. Flanders said something to the two boys separately and then raised his hand, clicking the stopwatch in it.

"Thirty seconds," said Flanders.

Scalder yelled from his corner: "Brown brother! Let's go to the movies and hold hands when we've patched up our spat!" Scalder's rapier wit. Succor Custis admitted no blacks to the movies.

Coffee looked empty. Vic thought his eyes were slightly rolled up in his head.

Suddenly a little black boy ran out of the north-wall crowd of black kids to Canning's corner. His clear little face was scared, and Vic couldn't make it out but it was clear the boy was scared for Canning. Canning's hard, clear face dissolved, and suddenly all the fear that was in the little boy was in Canning's face too. But then he composed himself quickly and just laid his right glove on the contour of the back of the boy's head. He stood up, and a girl who might have been the boy's sister snatched him back to the wall and whisked him back into the firehouse crowd. Vic guessed it was the boy this fight was about.

The boy would have nothing to fear, and not much to see. The fight was soon over. Coffee came out like a mantis, his hands held very high and agile, seeming to leave his flat belly exposed. Scalder could not touch him. Without ducking or feinting, he seemed to lean or turn to one side, and then those high-held fists unfurled like the crack of a roll-up window shade. Four of those five seconds and Scalder hit the floor, lights out, no blood spilled.

Vic's mouth was suddenly a housefly-hotel. Like everyone else's. Suddenly a black girl shouted:

"Mercy, Percy!" The black kids roared with laughter.

Then he heard the stranger's dry voice, a few inches from his ear:

"The Quality of Mercy Is Not Strained," he said. "Come get a milkshake at the Sonic?" Vic slid away, pretending he hadn't heard. Who was this guy? A Bounty Hunter? Had Coffee escaped or jumped bail?

Mrs. France and Flanders hurried into the ring to bend over Scalder. There had never been a stone-cold knockout in the firehouse. The crowd didn't know what to do with it. The black kids began to mill out as silently as the white people. They had half come for fun, testing the limits of a tolerance for their presence which wouldn't have existed for black adults. They were not taken seriously by the whites, and acted like they didn't care or want to be taken serious.

But Coffee wasn't going to make it easy on them either. Vic saw the silent, half-negro and half-oriental expression of will disappear, as if someone Else had paid the next month's rent on Coffee's face.

He danced around lightly and stuck out his open palm to the north wall.

"Hey, my brothers and sisters! Hey! Don't be shy! Where are the slaps of your fives on my five here? The blacksnake has defeated the rattlesnake! The Angus has trampled the Charolais! Where's my little brother? Here you are, child! If this bully was awake, wouldn't he want to shove you right back on the sidewalk and start our relationship over? Let's all go to the sidewalk!"

They had stopped. They were looking at him. And Vic could see them wondering if he was *really* somehow thinking he was black, or if he was mocking them. All the whites were staring too. Coffee had them by their eyeballs. Not that he appeared to notice.

He went quickly among the blacks, totally ignoring the whites; not a look. He started shaking hands and asking names, and they were giving them, and to each one he said, looking in their faces with conviction and intention that he would remember all their names, "I am Thomas 'Coffee' Canning," as if he were running for Governor. You could hear the quote marks around Coffee inflected in his voice with tiger-coat elegance. The black nebulae thus swirled out of the firehouse.

As Vic left the firehouse, the gray stranger approached again and silently handed him a card. "Call me if you want," he said. "I'd like to talk to you about a small newspaper I'm starting."

The plain white card read in small black letters, without address or phone information:

STILLMAN WHITING

CONGRESS OF RACIAL EQUALITY

Tad stuck it in his shirt pocket and they parted.

* * *

Ghost and Spook

Lorenzo Degree left the M-K-T switch station office with his checks for himself and Jane—a hundred dollars together for their 80 hours of work—and started across the tracks into Whitewright, his name for west of the tracks.

He looked north along the tracks and saw a huge yellow rail repair car parked up there on a side-rail. Six blacks were unloading cross ties. The engineer, an older black, was asleep in the engine compartment. Lorenzo could hear him snoring.

A gray Lincoln Continental halted on the dirt road. A light of delight switched on in the face of one of the crewmen. He'd been reading a beat up copy of Soul on Ice in the caboose that morning on break. Here, he thought, is my Amazon, come to collect her overqualified supermasculine menial for a better life of politics and stud service!

The electric window rolled down. A Howard University voice sang out in languid 100% silk: "Wander Waters. Come over here, Wander."

Lorenzo smiled. All the crew men smiled. It was the dream.

Wander's brooding and seething were those of a different Wander altogether. He forgot his panther's dignity, his statuesque bearing. His fantasy did not cloak himself in sunglasses, beret, 30 caliber grease gun. He danced as he walked, aware of men's eyes on him more than hers.

"When will you be off work, Wander?"

"Just now, sugar. I need to get clean for–"

"Yes, but not too clean!"

They all whistled and howled. Wander laughed. She said she'd pick him up in twenty minutes at Mr. Degree's. Lorenzo snorted to himself. The only tavern. east of the Kilnville tracks. The car sauntered away, down along the tracks towards Lorenzo, and turned past him. He looked in. She was not gorgeous, but prettier than plain, mocha and pure silk. She gave him a big smile, and Lorenzo looked away, wincing with pleasure.

There were three businesses east of the railyard.

Two were groceries, right across from one another at Oil Mill Hill's edge. Both were owned by whites. One of them kept 13 rhesus monkeys in a huge cage outside the entrance. All their customers were black.

Lorenzo went into Monkey Island Sundries, which was right on a long traffic island which separated two state highways. He bought a jar of peanut oil for his stiff right hand, which had been smashed by a tie two months before. He mixed the oil with Oil of Wintergreen.

Harry cashed his checks and gave him change. "Railroad checks are good as gold," said Harry, a former Weyerhaeuser forester from Hugo whose wife had inherited the store. Harry had introduced the monkeys.

"Yessir," said Harry, "No reflection on my clientele. I just love those rastus monkeys."

Harry said it to him about every other time he came in. He said it to every boy between 12 and 16 every week. Younger, it was wasted; older, it was faintly risky.

"Rhesus," said Lorenzo.

"Beg pardon?"

"The word is Rhesus. R-h-e-s-u-s. Rhymes with ceases and pieces. Not with Jesus."

"Beg Pardon, beg pardon," said Harry silkily.

Lorenzo wanted a 7-up, but Harry was slow and his sister Jane needed their paychecks first. Thursday she went to the bank, to avoid the Friday rush.

Lorenzo's father William Degree owned the third business in Oil Mill, a restaurant since '58, also a tavern. They lived next door in a two-story house with white pillars. There were four acres, with a giant garden in the back. If it had been lifted whole and deposited next door to Monticello, it would have slipped in as smoothly as page 473 of *War and Peace* fits between 472 and 474.

It had taken ten years to bring it back alive. The Willkies had abandoned it as their local palace when the railroad came in and a subdivision was needed for the sudden influx of blacks into all-white Kilnville. They had abandoned it with austere public-spiritedness, though in 1910 it had been only 11 years old. McKinley Grant Willkie finished growing up in Peace Street.

They had refused to sell it until deterioration reduced its grandness to a level suitable to its vicinity.

William bought it in 1954 and he and his brother Jean-Claude, a master carpenter, restored it themselves, preserving all the dovetail mortises and tenons, tuckpointing the brick foundation, jacking up headers, burning off layers of wallpaper, scraping, sanding, rewiring and replumbing.

Lorenzo and Jane were three when it was bought; by age five they were helping with small tasks, and painting by age seven.

Jane was not in the house, so Lorenzo went over to the restaurant. When he entered, his father was sitting in a booth with an adding machine and a large stack of receipts, which he was uncharacteristically ignoring. His thin dark face, the more creased blueprint from which Lorenzo's was drawn, was impassive but fully attentive.

Four players from the visiting Ravia Panthers semipro ball club had untouched hamburgers at the table. Jane was at the counter, talking in low tones to a white boy.

Lorenzo stared. His stare was added to the other five stares.

The white boy was about five nine, same as Lorenzo. He wore baggy black trousers and a large white shirt whose short sleeves were rolled high up on his slender sculpted biceps. The clothes were old but starched and very clean. The shoes were well preserved white bucs, about four years out of style. The boy did not turn his head.

"I am pleased to meet you. May I add your name and handshake to those of Mr. And Miss Degree, Mr. Cross, Mr. Greene, Mr. Thomas and Mr. Thwaite?"

Lorenzo sucked in his breath. The accent was black as beauty.

It was educated black, but southern, not northern. There was not a drop of mockery or parody in it. He closed his eyes briefly and replayed its flow in his mind's ear as the stranger approached and shook his hand. The white boy talked in color.

Lorenzo noticed that he had at once thought of the stranger as a man rather than a boy, though he couldn't have been much older than Lorenzo's 15. Not with those narrow smooth arms.

"Reply, son," said William Degree. Lorenzo recouped himself instantly, still shaking the pale hand.

"Lorenzo Degree."

The boy turned to the counter stool. "Pleased to meet you, Lorenzo. I am Thomas 'Coffee' Canning."

He shut his eyes as if he was going into a trance, and placed the tips of his fingers together at waist level. The tips of the fingers he moved apart and together in quick alternation. He spoke mockingly, pretending to be in contact with the Other World.

"You have some questions. These clothes make you wonder, What year has he come from?" He dropped his hand and opened his eyes. Lorenzo looked around at his father and sister, who were no help. They were looking away deliberately.

"Stringtown Reformatory for six years. I entered there in a 10 year old's jeans and shirt. These unclaimed clothes were in their lost and found. I have only been home two weeks, so I have no other clothes that fit. Please don't feel awkward or embarrassed. Your curiosity is natural."

Lorenzo tried to keep his face neutral as his father's.

"Where do you live, Thomas?"

"I go by Coffee, and I expect to keep living in a local manse."

"What is a manse?"

"It's a parsonage, Lorenzo," said William.

"Too true," said Coffee.

"Your daddy is a preacher?" asked Lorenzo. "What church?"

Circling in, just circling in slowly like Perry Mason, like a buzzard.

Coffee seemed to be utterly relaxed. Lorenzo wanted to get up and look under the counter, or feel the lips of the baseballers, to see if there was some ventriloquy happening. The black hair was wavy, but the skin was marble and the eyes were green algae.

He shook his head. "I been sent home with Canning since January. He is the minister of the Golgotha Baptist Church. You afraid to ask what I did? I'm not ashamed to tell you." But then he did not just say. He looked out the window, eyes rolling and brooding with their green shining like a cat's in the dark, then looked back at his food. Still silence.

William Degree said, "What matters is what you are, not what you did." But he said it with a questioning chill in his tone.

Coffee's eyes showed a little heat. He had picked up the emphasis William put on the word "are." Lorenzo looked at the boy, thinking: not slow; knows signs.

Coffee was trying to burn a hole with his eye in William's face, whose left eyebrow remained steadily and slightly lifted, as it had when he spoke.

Jane was thinking that the three of them, William, Lorenzo and Coffee, had the same build. In silhouette, the process which subtracted color, they could have been triplets. She thought of the Abraham Lincoln silhouette which hung next to the daguerreotype of Frederick Douglass over the cast-iron Adams Mantel in their living room.

"I shot the man who said he was my father. His name was Ray Scarberry. Man was not my father." Coffee's voice was losing its education.

"He never called me my real name, Thomas. Know what he called me?"

It was rhetorical, but Coffee looked at them all, ending and holding on Jane, and waited. And waited, turning angry eyes on each of them. And waited. She thought, Looney in a bus station.

She half-laughed and shrugged. "No, what?" she said

"Nig."

They waited. Again he didn't elaborate. The eyes moving around fast again, boring in hard.

"Why Nig?" asked Jane. Where was Lorenzo's tongue, or William's?

"He said it gave me something high to shoot for." And Coffee laughed.

"He made me clean out the outhouse with my bare hands. Said he couldn't afford to let it get on his shovel. That was one of my good jobs.

"We slept in the same room. He used to take a bowie knife a foot long to bed with my mama every night. Said he needed to make sure she was sincere in her lovin'." Coffee laughed again, shaking his head, rolling his green eyes.

"She wasn't. So one night he used it. But not the point, oh nothin' so bad. Just took some shavin's with the edge."

"Holy ghost," muttered Lorenzo. Jane thought she might like to tame the air with her female voice; if the air in there was a horse, it was sure bucking.

Coffee said, "So I blew his foot off in his bed."

"His foot?" exclaimed Lorenzo.

"I was a kid. I never shot his gun before." He looked indignant.

"They sent you to Stringtown for that?"

"He didn't die. They believed him over me. He said he'd whipped me for stealing Jonah Smicka's rooster. He even made a big show of returning Jonah's rooster. Jonah didn't even have a rooster. But he took it and said nothing. If a Scarberry gives you a rooster or a whipping, you just take it.

"Didn't your mom speak up?"

"Still scared of him. Hard not to be after what he did to her neck. He liked to tie his traitors to a pickup and drag them around for a few hours. That's what he called his enemies, traitors."

"So how'd you wind up in Reverend Canning?"

"He went to Stringtown and asked them for the meanest kid there." Coffee smiled again. They couldn't tell if he was kidding.

"Are you going to live up to that honor?"

Coffee smiled a huge smile fill of strikingly large but perfect teeth, a smile as black as burning coals.

"Proud of that. No honk ride me or train my mouth to take no bit."

The accent had switched smooth as tracks in the switchyard. Now it switched back again. "But in Stringtown I learned a lot about my background and my duties to my people. There I learned to read and write and think, thanks to my brothers there. I can assure you, there is not a person on earth who has a thing in the world I want, or would not ask for rather than take."

"You have the speech of a preacher," William noted, wry.

"Thank you sir. I did not always. I have great respect for Reverend Canning, who lent me his name, as all of us have been lent our names." Now his eyes were looking up and his words were unctuous and all of them wondered if this could be for real. The spell Coffee'd woven was beginning to split at the knees.

Jane asked, "What you mean, lent our names?"

"You know where Degree comes from?" Suddenly he was a contemptuous know-it-all.

Lorenzo said, "It's French. De Gris is Grayhair, or could be from the town called Gray. Our people are from Louisiana." Rudely twisting his head, ultra-skeptical, Coffee looked at William, who nodded confirmation.

"Well. Yet you aren't French. And you're from nowhere named Grayhair; and you are very black. Nothing Grayish about you. The name does not describe you, or tell you what town you came from, or reflect your tribe of people, which are the three ways they used to hand out names to people."

The four ballplayers had had enough. As in not touching with 10 foot poles. Their burgers half-eaten, they rose, cleared their throats, paid, clattered out the screen door of the restaurant in their cleats.

Then Lorenzo said, "Our great Uncle says that his grandfather was named Lorenze and spoke French. They say Pirate Lafitte sold him to some Choctaws who strapped boards to their foreheads to make them flat. And these Choctaws sold him to some white planters who lived outside of Baton Rouge where they grew rice and cotton. They called him De Gris because he tuned gray when he was in his twenties, and because he was old and strong and smart enough to lead the others up here among the Indians when the war ended. De Gris meant that he was smart as an elder man."

"I want to order a barbecued beef sandwich and some iced tea," said Coffee impatiently, looking at Jane.

"OK," said Lorenzo, relieved despite Coffee's rudeness, moving now behind the counter to the gas range. "Hot sauce or mild?"

"Hot."

Great, thought Jane. My brother picks now to put zeal into his work. I am left closest to this ugly duckling whose face is not as ugly as his mouth.

"White sugar in your tea?" she asked. Lorenzo grinned, but Coffee seemed oblivious to her humor, until he spoke again.

"I am not caucasian," Coffee announced in a sharp, clear tone, as if he were calling a password to a sentry as a battlefield position. "I realized at Stringtown that my parents had hidden the fact that my real daddy was a black man, but nature has left my color out. I used to think I was an albino."

"You're no albino," Jane said, taking from Lorenzo the blue plate of barbecue stacked on a caraway roll. "An albino has pink eyes, and you can see all his blood vessels in his skin. His hair is white." She handed him a roll. The now-aproned Lorenzo at the grill and William Degree on his feet by his booth looked at her like deer listening closely in a forest.

"I now know this," Coffee answered instantly. "I call myself black. I call myself Coffee because my black soul and my white skin make me add up to Coffee with cream. My Great-Great-Grandfather was also a slave, owned by a Creek Indian tribesman in Sapulpa. I don't think anyone here would want to say that I am a white man, when they know now from what I have told them that I am black."

The door opened and the photo negative of Charles Atlas came in. Jane groaned at the sight of Wander Waters. "Oh, Brother Coffee," she muttered to herself, "you just gave the devil his cue."

Wander was shirtless and sweatless despite the raw heat which at 5:30 was still quavering over the blacktop outside.

He picked up a heavy wrought iron chair and held it like a book of matches.

"Fee Fi Fo Fum," said Wander, sniffing exaggeratedly.

William Degree walked over to Wander, very close.

"There are no colorless personnel in attendance at present," said William bemusedly. "This is Master Coffee Canning, Negro, who just moved over to Whitewright."

Coffee turned on the stool then, and said, "Thank you for offering to hold my chair while I sit down. But I am already seated."

Lorenzo burst out laughing. Jane howled. Wander stared.

"Wander, you looked like a weasel who'd caught a skunk when he thought he stole a chicken!" cried Jane. O Jesus, lighten him up, she thought. This is no stage play.

Wander ignored her. The cold challenge in his expression remained. Nor did he lower the chair.

"Brother," said Coffee levelly, chewing barbecue, "do you know how much Indian blood it takes to be a full restricted Indian in the USA?"

"A river of blood would not make you my brother. Don't call me brother, ghost."

"One fourth. But how much blood, Spook, did it take to be a slave under the laws?"

The chair whipped down toward Coffee, who twisted and leaped from the chair quick as a fly, landing on his feet with no loss of breath:

"If you are not my brother, you're no black, just a spook. A black recognizes his brothers . . . . Maybe an eighth, you think? No, just a drop, if the line was straight. An excuse. One Sixty Fourth. Or less.

The chair had stopped just short of smashing to bits over the top of the stool; Wander's huge forearm bulged. It was as stunning exhibit of strength and control as was Coffee's move of speed and agility and jive.

"I know about drops," said Wander coldly. "Haj Elijah relates that all men are brothers. Allah made the black man with whites in his eyes and a red tongue in his mouth. He made the red man with whites in his eyes and black hair. But he made the white devils only with blacks in their pupils and skin that changes colors, from black evil to red blushing shame to green bile to yellow fear. The white devil's skin is the map of his soul which we are to read and beware. They look like men, but they are a different breed, and not our brothers. They steal their false colors from drops of blood they have spilled.

"I think, leech, you'd better leave," Wander continued softly.

Coffee half crouched, burning his eyes hard into Wander's swinging his arms from side to side in front of him like a monkey as he spoke rhythmically.

"I know about Haj Elijah," Coffee said. His eyes rolled up. "He also tells the story about doves and crows. The crows and doves were eating bugs in a field. The crows hit a patch where there used to be cotton, and they all ate cotton seeds. Doves, just as mean as crows, really, were over on the other side, and they hit a patch of eggplants. They really liked 'em, and ate all the eggplants, which are full of soft seeds that go down smooth. Haj Elijah said that usually seeds go into gizzard, but these seeds just went straight into their hearts, they were so smooth. Pretty soon those eggplants started growin' inside those doves, swellin' like eggplants do. And pretty soon those cotton bolls swelled up inside the crows. One day they all busted at the same time, and the crows were white as cotton, and the doves were black as eggplants. So watch out for what might be growin' under the skin.

"I think, dovey-boy, I'll stay where I belong."

"I think you'd both better leave my store," said William. "I don't cotton much to your Jim Crow bedtime stories." Wander looked at Coffee.

"After you, massa," he said.

"Much obliged, cousin," said Coffee cheerily. Lorenzo groaned aloud melodramatically, wringing his apron.

William looked at Jane. "Who's Haj Elijah?"

Jane said, "I don't know."

Lorenzo said, "It's not Little Richard." Little Richard had been a Christian evangelist singing only Gospel since abandoning rock and roll in 1957.

William went over to his booth and sat down. Jane said, "Daddy! What's Wander going to do to that boy?"

"I don't know. Go see. If it's not in here, it's not my business."

Lorenzo was at the door, motionless. A wasp was buzzing around him like a mad jay; he ignored it. Jane looked out. There was Wander's new Dallas girlfriend, shaking Wander's face, pounding on Wander's amazing chest. Picking up his thick arms that even in unconsciousness could never be limp. She stood up, dusted off her business suit, and stared down at him through her smart sunglasses, her dark face impassive. "Well, shit," she said, in an exact elegant tone which would go with Goodness Gracious. She got in her Lincoln and drove away. Coffee had vanished.

"Call the ambulance," said Lorenzo wonderingly, and went out to Wander's carcass. Jane ignored his injunction, following him out. They stood over him. Wander groaned.

"What was it, knucks? piece of chain?" asked Lorenzo.

Wander tried to talk, but there was something funny about his jaw. "Ist," he mumbled.

"What?" they asked.

"Ist!" said Wander, clenching his fist and raising it. "E it me wi is Ist. Boke ma djaw heah," he said, holding his jaw.

"Gone like a ghost," said William. "Maybe you were right, Wander," he laughed.

* * *

Imitation of Coffee

Another thing I can do is run, thought Vic. I can run faster than Jackass Scalder who is after me. What I smoke in those Bugler papers is not ugly Tobacco, it's Mullein. Now mullein is your excellent herb, says Tad and the Old Wives I can't believe he reads. After all he writes about seas of sludge and Mr. Malthus and a black nation carved out of Mississippi and Alabama. But Mullein?! He says it strengthens the lungs, sac by sac. So I smoke that, and I do run like a nylon hose.

Vic thought about Lorenzo as he walked to the theater.

"Proposed," Lorenzo had said, "that this here Willkie boy is so pleased to see a certain Scalder eat dust for once, inasmuch as said loser has been scalding Master Willkie's bottom in recent days."

Vic had reddened down to his roots. "Proposed," he reported bitterly, "that I like shooting rats with a BB gun with you in the dump a lot better than shooting bull with you in the firehouse."

Lorenzo laughed easily. "Let back a quarter turn on the screw. What are you going to do to celebrate?"

"Scalder will get worse. You think when he wakes up he'll See The Light? Start a set of callouses on his bended knee?"

"Where you going?"

"Movie."

"I went to one of those once."

"Knock it off."

Lorenzo did not smile. "It was a cartoon festival, featuring Felix the Cat. He had a diamond mine in South Africa and the Professor was trying to steal it from him by tricking him with a mirage machine."

"No foolin'."

"I'm not."

"That's too good to be true."

"The only movie I ever saw in Kilnville."

"How'd you get in?"

"Don't you remember when Succor cut a hole in the wall and let us sit in folding chairs in the very back?"

"Yeah." They'd been a remote dark noise. Cups and popcorn flew out like bats, shrieking with laughter.

"Catman," third-grade-Vic has asked the Whiz at the rink once, "why do they call them coons?"

"Well, they're scared to come out except at night, and they got white eyes inside black circles, and they always trying to wash the black out of their skin, just like raccoons." Vic believed all that at the time, just like he believed they story everybody told about how Billy Strofford was pregnant.

"Oh my God," said Vic.

"What?" said Lorenzo.

"Shame memory."

"Winces don't mend fences," said Lorenzo. If you heard him at school, thought Vic, he always talked mockingbird to the teachers like someone out of Uncle Remus. Do declare. Don't say. Sho is a delightable mornin'. Sine X + Cosine Z. "'What?'" Better climba tree than Gee omlettry. Etc.

Then he struck you out one time, next time gave you a fat one to hit because he liked you in particular right then. He didn't think it was fair. Then he debated your socks off and sustained the proposition that Today, Karl Marx Would Not Be A Communist. He never gave you an inch in a race; he'd give you a head start, put a pebble in his shoe, strap his arms to his sides, or run backwards. And still win.

Vic remembered the first time he ever talked to Lorenzo. Tad had set Vic to mowing the overgrown flower beds outside the walls, and mulching and fertilizing with cow manure. Cars that drove by with friends' parents stopped, talked. In his lonely daydreams, that is. Vic was proud and eager to be seen. At work. Wielding a spade, sweating genuine sweat. Maybe a girl would pass, stop. Which would it be? And the cravings would start flooding out of him, firing in his mind like smoking guns.

Who would care to be surprised and learn about the real Gene Victor, rebel democrat, founder of rugged Gene Victorism? Who would find him remarkable and beautiful? Lorenzo passed by, bound home from school.

Lorenzo. Said. Just. What. Vic. Daydreamed. Hearing. Someone. Say. He could tell Vic wasn't stuck up because he was rich. He wasn't afraid to dirty his hands in dirt. "You could be aristocratic, with the money you've got. But you're not."

Whenever Lorenzo would say just what you wanted to hear most, in your daydreams, you always heard the real truth behind it. The praise tempted out the fact of your conceitedness or shallowness or callowness, or whatever warm slick sentiment inspired your daydreams. Lorenzo was not dumb or insincere. There was no standing his praise. It was Midas' touch; it turned you into gold.

Don't ask how much Lorenzo knew what he was doing all along. You knew he knew. You also knew he wasn't sucking ass, and you also knew he wasn't dumb, or scared, or ingratiating. Too much ease, too many unsuspecting moments of solemnity when he thought no one was watching him—too smart in school, too solid. His ironic praise was the subtlest and gentlest of ironies, underneath which he was real.

Now they began walking toward the wide bay doors.

"Well," said Vic finally, "I'm not wincing. I'm just grimacing."

"Yeah, man," said Lorenzo, absently. He was looking down the street after the receding crowd of Coffee and the Children of Hamelin. "Looks like they're going to see a flick, like you."

"Yeah, man!" laughed Vic.

Yeah, they used to go down to the dump and shoot rats with BB gun. It was Lorenzo's. Lakota said she'd buy Vic one when he brought home a live green crow, and Tad said he'd buy him one the very day he found a black tulip growing in their beds.

"Never City, man," groaned Vic. "Never my own piece, man."

Lorenzo laughed. "You're tall, black haired, dark skinned, you look like Ray Danton in *The Rise and Fall of Legs Diamond*. Another dancer pinin' for a gun. Here, I saw a rat behind that dead battery. Shoot the battery, the acid might catch the rat."

"Magnificent, Lorenzo. So sporting." Vic took the gun, waited, shot. The rat flipped in the air and fell dead on top of the Diehard.

"I thought you never went to a movie, Vic."

"Don't much. We get channel 12 at home."

"Ray Danton is to me what Felix the Cat is to you. Does what he likes, is the cool thing that he is, and Honey Swat Key Melt You Pahnts!"

"Honi soit qui mal y pense!"

"Hey, Sir Willkie, I got an idea," mused Lorenzo. Instantly Vic grew wary.

"Yeah?"

"Let's go to that movie too. I surmise Coffee is up to making another scene."

* * *

Vic's Diary, June 14, 1961

Today I went over to Degree's house, up past the rhesus monkey cages, and I came up to that old mansion with the mighty oaks painted white four feet up, and the limestones painted lime green like an eye joke along the smooth dirt path to the oak boarded front porch, and I knocked as hard as I could, I being the postcard of the young rich man come to call at poor angel beauty's home.

"Get on away from here, Victor Willkie! You're trespassing by trudging up to our porch!" came her voice, just as black as her skin is and mine should be.

"Well I will, Jane Deborah Degree, if you will tell me why your father and mother have decorated your yard like the McAlester prison grounds which I have seen."

Tad had visited the State Pen for four years, spreading revolution in the guise of a minister, which Jane knew first hand, Tad having visited her cousin Jeffrey there once a month for a year when he did time for stealing a $20 propane bottle he in fact never stole.

"Our minds are spotless, and yours proves dingy," Jane retorted. "On the score of color and on the score of motive, you don't belong here. Get!"

Tad had traveled to peculiar spots during his provocateur stint, when Oklahomans tried rebellion and learned they didn't cotton to it. He lugged us with him to the Hopi reservation, making it seem light and easy, though my sister and I fought like cobra and mongoose as was our rule.

Why were we going? As always, out dad with the 100% lean mind was ready to make fluff sound like steak. "I've heard they get cucumber spirits and corncob devils to knock some peace into their hotshots," he said. "If a lot of old women can do that, maybe I can learn something."

We pulled into a tourist center and ate some posole-lamb stew with frybread, then we drove on in to Hotevilla Third Mesa, the westernmost of Hopi towns. Tad pulled into a side street in front of a small house, and just sat there. The rest of us were sweating 30 seconds after he turned off the motor, but not Tad. In 30 more, my sister and I were screaming at one another over partitioning the last bottle of 7-up. Suddenly an older woman came out of the house and waved her wrist briskly at us, shouting "Get! Get!" and then went back in, apparently satisfied we would quickly get. Which abashed us kids decisively. Secretly we'd been hungry for something personal, supernatural around any deceptively ordinary corner.

Tad left the reservation at once. He'd gotten what he came for. He was always going long distances to find out what he already knew; but he just had to come see it work, he said.

We ate corn and cucumbers from the prison garden patch every day that summer.

And the second time Jane said to get, I got.

I love corn. But I am not corny. My heart is as lean of sentiment as my Dad's is of fluff. I am serious.

What bird loves corn the best? The crow.

The thin man inside Tad is not trying to get out. You can see he's running things backstage the minute he appears.

I am thin, taking after my mother, Lakota. I think I must be more complicated, or else the facts themselves are more complex. My insides are a lot more opaque than Dad's. But I remember the very morning, in the Huckins Hotel in Oklahoma City, when I realized that beneath my pale skin, I am black as a new moon sky.

I was 13 then. But even back when I was 8, I knew I was not wasp. They had a photo portrait made of me at Curtis Studios. We were at the hotel when the portrait was delivered.

My lips and hands in the oil looked Semitic to me. They said I was pure British Isle, but suddenly I was convinced that I had been adopted, and that my lost parents were Turkish Jews. I was Saul, this revelation was Damascus Crossing; now I was Paul.

But then I took in more data in my dreams. Which would show me my big old soul every time. I could spot my soul among the crowds of other figures by the fixed looks it would give me. I was in New Orleans in one, and ran into a crowd of men on a street corner. One, slender and young, looked at me with his white eyes smoldering in their black sockets, just stood and looked. Liar, his eyes called me, and might have said, you do not have to lift up a rock to find me. I'm fully visible behind the film of tears on your eyes at all times, just under the peeling whitewash on your skin.

I thought I'd been hunting for some friend in the dream. The black I am let me know he was not hiding.

"Spirits talk to me," I told Jane on my third try as I fell in beside her just after she passed the rhesus cages. I'd stood in wait for her after she'd crossed the tracks, knowing the danger if I fell in with her in sight of Whitewright.

"They do?" more than she'd been willing to say. Her voice could turn from green leaves to lead and tin in a nanosecond. "What do they tell Madame Victor?"

"They say that the reason the rhesus monkeys always fall silent when you pass me in their presence is not only your obvious dignity."

"Well, why do they?" They in fact did, but did they also quiet for her when I wasn't there? Did they for others? Perhaps my spirit guide insight was flakily based. But I pressed on with authority.

"Because they can't figure out if you're my shadow or I'm yours."

Jim Drummond is a criminal defense lawyer in Norman, Oklahoma. He earned a Master's in Creative Writing at the City College of New York, mentored by Donald Barthelme and Frederic Tuten, and has published fiction and poetry in small magazines and anthologies. His earlier days as a tank driver, drover in a cattle sale barn, murderer of mesquite trees with chainsaws and pesticides now banned everywhere, and deliverer of submarine sandwiches, likely had zero qualitative effect on his literary production, but their quantitative effect has been immeasurable. He is married to Deborah King Drummond, a certified clinical hypnotherapist. A visit to their home would confirm that they prefer eccentricity in all creatures.

www.ingramcontent.com/pod-product-compliance
Lightning Source LLC
Chambersburg PA
CBHW060330260626
47160CB00007B/2759